# *Phone Calls From Heaven*

# *Phone Calls From Heaven*

## C. J. Plogger

RESOURCE *Publications* • Eugene, Oregon

PHONE CALLS FROM HEAVEN

Resource Publications
An Imprint of Wipf and Stock Publishers
199 W. 8th Ave., Suite 3
Eugene, OR 97401

www.wipfandstock.com

PAPERBACK ISBN: 978-1-6667-3698-4
HARDCOVER ISBN: 978-1-6667-9598-1
EBOOK ISBN: 978-1-6667-9599-8

JANUARY 4, 2022 3:07 PM

This book is dedicated to the Byrge family—
Mike, Karen, and Malachi.
They are true lifelong friends who make our lives better.

# *Thank You!*

Thank you Fran Allred and Mickey Johnson of We Edit Books for their expertise and patience.

Thank you to my wife, Janeen, for first believing and second for being with me.

# *One*

K AREN'S mind was preoccupied as she gripped the long, curved handle of her Hoover vacuum cleaner maneuvering it over the light beige carpeting of the family room. The family room was a fortress for the Byrges. A 65-inch large screen Sony television was affixed to one wall just eight feet from the L shaped brown suede couches that were well used. Karen mused how messy the boys were as the vacuum cleaner loudly sucked in broken pieces of potato chips and loose unpopped kernels of Orville Redenbacher's popcorn.

Karen ran through a mental list of what she had to do and kept silently repeating to herself not to get overwhelmed but remain calm, it would all get done. Once she finished cleaning up after her husband, Mike and son, Malachi, she had several other projects to complete. She had to go to the courthouse and pay their property taxes, stop by the Post Office and pick up a birthday package sent by her parents, go grocery shopping, take some clothes that Malachi had outgrown over to a friend's house, and she made a commitment to help set up for a blood drive at the church.

Mike and Malachi stayed up late the previous night watching the Cincinnati Reds pull out a narrow victory over their rivals, the St. Louis Cardinals, in extra innings. As the athletic tension played out on the large screen before them, drinks and snacks spilled and flung from the grip of the excited spectators as they fervently cheered on their team, the Reds. Exuberant groans and enthusiastic applause ricocheted through the room depending on how their team was doing.

At 11:00 p.m., before she settled into slumber, Karen popped her head into the family room and firmly warned the rambunctious observers to be careful and not to make a mess as she didn't have time tomorrow to clean their carnage. Both Mike and Malachi feigned a hurt look, "We would never make a mess, you know us."

"Yes, I do know you and that's why I'm warning you. Plus, it's a school night, so don't be up late."

In unison, they robotically responded with Mike saying, "Yes, dear," and Malachi remarking, "Yes, Mom."

The next day she remembered their promise of not making a mess as she planned how she was going to accomplish all she needed to get done. Just as she was pushing the roaring vacuum cleaner over one last patch of the carpet, her thoughts abruptly screeched to a halt as she heard a musical ring tone blaring from her Samsung cellphone.

"What now?" Karen thought as she pushed the on/off switch of the vacuum cleaner and became tangled in the long, stretchy, vinyl suction hose. Lurching forward, almost tripping, she freed herself from the clutches of the elastic hose and walked toward the coffee table which still had remnants of diet Dr. Pepper spilled on it from the soiree of the previous night.

She knew that the incoming call was from her son, Malachi, because his ringtone was the energetic song, One Short Day, from the Broadway musical, Wicked. On one of their vacations, the Byrge family traveled to New York City, rode the subway, settled into their seats in the metropolitan iconic Broadway theater, and enjoyed the grand production.

"Hey honey, what's going on? Aren't you supposed to be in class?"

With an exasperated tone, Malachi snapped. "I'm walking to class but I don't have the history report that was due today."

"O.K., why don't you have it?"

"Because you didn't remind me to grab it off of the dining table."

"Oh, I didn't remind you to take your report?"

"Well, I need it. If I don't turn it in today, it will hurt my grade in Mr. Robert's class. You have to bring it to me!"

Karen quickly ran through the multitude of undone tasks in her mind. "Honey, I'm not sure if I have time today to stop by the school."

"That's not fair, it won't take that long. You're not that busy today. I need that paper."

"O.K., I am extremely busy today but I will bring your report. What time do you need it?"

"History is at 2:00, don't be late," Malachi ordered and then quickly said, "I have to go," as the line went silent.

Karen slowly moved the phone away from her ear. "Bye honey, I love you too."

As Karen walked into the dining room, she saw the multi-paged history report laying forsaken on the white tablecloth draped over the wooden table. She picked it up and thumbed through it noticing it was about the Civil War Battle of Antietam. She shook her head side to side and thought, "First, they stay up too late watching a baseball game and now it's my fault he forgot his assignment."

When Karen returned to the family room, she glanced up at one of the wood framed family pictures hanging on the wall and looked at Malachi. She reminisced, "He was so young then, now tomorrow, he will be sixteen years old. Where has the time gone?" Then snapping out of her nostalgic spell, Karen started calculating how she was going to get everything finished and take Malachi's paper to him.

Karen looked at the clock and methodically started timing each of her activities to set up an orderly agenda. "If I go now and drop off the clothes, I can be at the courthouse in twenty minutes and that will probably take a half hour. Then I should be able to stop and pick up the present and then I can spend an hour at the church helping set up so I can get his report to him a little after 1:00."

Karen was glad that she had her day mapped out and hoped nothing out of the ordinary would arise but she was greatly mistaken. Snatching Malachi's report from the table, clutching her black leather purse in hand as she dug through it to find her keys, and balancing a stuffed box of clothes, Karen was now in motion.

First stop, her friend's house to drop off the cardboard bundle now resting next to her in the passenger seat and then off to the courthouse. Karen smiled as she handed her friend, Janeen Steele, the clothes and rapidly fired off, "Can't stay, I have a lot of things to get done today and have to go to the school to bring Malachi a report he forgot. Call me later and we'll go to Starbucks."

Holding the brown container of hand me down pants and shirts, Janeen chuckled, "Thank you. Good luck getting everything done. You know our kids don't think we're busy at all, do they?"

"Isn't that the truth? See you soon."

Next stop, the courthouse. Normally, there weren't many people waiting at the assessor's office to pay their taxes but today was an exception. Karen mumbled to herself, "It will be all right. This will take a little longer than I thought but everything will get done. I will save the day by getting my son's report to him."

Karen smiled as she imagined herself running into Anderson High School holding the history report elevated in the air loudly exclaiming, "Malachi, I am here and have brought your report. No need to thank me. I am just doing my duty as Super Mom." As she patiently stood in line, Karen's mind designed her red and blue Super Mom cape and thought about the accessories she would wear to accentuate it.

Karen was yanked back into reality when she heard, "Sir, this is the amount you owe and I'm sorry that you don't agree with it but you have to pay it."

Veins bulged from the irate man's neck and Karen thought he was going to explode. "I'm not going to pay it because it's highway robbery."

ONE

Karen wanted to bypass the lengthy line and tell the animated man, "I'll pay it for you. Please just get out of the way because I have a lot to do today." But she didn't.

After a few parting shots, the man left in a huff and slowly, the line dissipated and Karen was able to pay their taxes. Now to pick up the present, the church, then the school where the anxious Malachi was awaiting his report.

Fortunately, Karen was able to quickly pick up the birthday present and drive to the church. It was now almost noon so Karen could spend an hour helping set up chairs and tables for the Red Cross blood drive. She enjoyed helping at the church and felt strongly about serving for such a worthy cause.

Lots of laughter was mixed in with the task of carrying chairs and setting up tables. Several volunteers showed up and Karen was happy they would be finished in an hour. An hour flew by and Karen paused to view the layout of their labor. "Now to the school and then I can go grocery shopping and get everything done before the boys get home."

Standing next to her white Ford Escort, Karen fished her phone out of her bulky purse and texted Malachi. "I'm headed to the school now and should be there about 1:25. Where can I meet you?"

A small icon flashed on her screen alerting Karen that Malachi had responded. "In front of the gym and hurry. What's taking you so long?"

Karen smiled as she thought back to the picture of Malachi she looked at earlier in their family room and reflected, "He wasn't so snippy back in those days. Then, he wanted Mommy to be with him every second of the day." Still, she loved him and Mike with all of her heart.

Mike had caught Karen's eye in the lobby of the bank where she worked as a teller right after college. She hoped he would end up at her window instead of the three other tellers that might have completed his transaction. Mike seemed preoccupied as he slid the check to Karen underneath the small Plexiglass partition. Karen

5

noticed he quickly withdrew his hand as if she was going to snatch it and pull him towards her.

Without much eye contact, Mike took the cash Karen counted out and lowered his head as he barely mumbled, "Thank you very much." Karen professionally responded in kind but internally she was happy and pleased to have met him. For the rest of her shift, in between checking balances and doling out money from deposit slips, she found herself thinking about him.

Finally, her shift was over and as Karen was walking toward her car in the parking lot, she noticed Mike standing nearby. She was surprised but quickly came to her senses when he shyly approached her, "Excuse me, but you helped me today and I'm sorry I was a little nervous."

"You don't have to apologize but why were you nervous?"

Mike looked down at the ground. "Well, normally when I go to the bank, I don't see beautiful tellers like you."

"Oh my."

"Would you go out to dinner with me sometime?"

Karen was slightly taken back by his forthrightness, but courage filled her heart. "Sure, that would be nice. When would you like to go?"

"Since I'm on a roll, I'm going to keep going," as a huge grin spread across his face, "what about tonight?"

Karen looked Mike up and down, found herself amazed with his boldness, and shocked herself when she replied, "I would love to go out tonight."

"You would? Where would you like to go?"

Karen loved Mexican food and suggested, La Ranchero, which was a quaint festive place where the spicy salsa melted in your mouth. At the brightly colored restaurant, the walls were covered with vibrant orange and cloud-like blue paint, Karen and Mike talked and laughed and found themselves wanting to spend more time together.

The main reason why Karen and Mike were attracted to each other was their love for God. Both of them were saved at an early age. Karen remembered walking down a dusty aisle in between folding metal chairs at a summer camp and kneeling at a rickety altar. Mike went to a revival after a friend invited him and the hopeful words of the exuberant evangelist resonated in his spirit and he accepted the Lord.

Both Karen and Mike graduated from Anderson University, she with an accounting degree and he with an education degree with an emphasis on special needs students. Karen was casually submitting applications to accounting firms but didn't mind working at the bank so she enjoyed the privilege of being selective of which job she would pursue.

Mike started teaching at Anderson High School where he was living out his dream of making a difference in the lives of students. Much later, when Malachi ventured out of junior high school and was promoted to high school, he and his dad would be in same school building.

Karen and Mike started seeing each other regularly and the other bank tellers mercilessly teased Karen with these words, "That guy is here to see you again." Karen's eyes would swell and she responded, "That's not just any guy, that's my guy."

After eight months of courting, a date for them to marry was set and Mike nervously stood in front of a church building. Tears flowed from his eyes while his bride in a flowing white dress slowly promenaded toward him. Since both of them were working and with Karen's impeccable financial training and skills, they were able to buy a house on Scarlet Drive not long after they gazed into each other's eyes and said, "I do."

Two years later, Karen was patting Mike's knee at the gynecologist's office urging him to relax as he wanted to pace back and forth. Finally, the gum chewing receptionist, sitting in her faux leather chair, reached up and slid the glass window partition aside and told them they could go to Room #8. What seemed an eternity to both of them came to be a celebratory occasion when the older, whitehaired doctor announced that Karen was going to have a baby.

As Karen was driving toward the school to give the elusive history report to Malachi, pleasant memories flooded through her mind about him. Karen found herself getting a little emotional as she pondered the fact that her baby would be turning sixteen years old tomorrow. First, she didn't want to admit that she was getting older and second, the cliché that children grow up so fast was more accurate than she realized.

It was 1:17 p.m. and the rectangular yellow traffic signal flashed a green arrow and Karen began turning right from Scatterfield Road to travel east on 53rd Street toward the school.

This intersection is surrounded with a McDonalds to the northeast, a busy Sheetz gas station to the northwest, a Taco Bell to the southwest, and a CVS pharmacy to the southeast. Hundreds of vehicles enter Anderson after exiting U.S. 69 to create a constant continuum of rushing traffic in this area. Farther down the road, there are several department stores, restaurants, and specialty businesses making this intersection the most chaotic and dangerous one in Anderson.

When Karen was in the middle of the perilous juncture, she didn't see the massive Kenworth W900A semi-trailer, filled to maximum capacity, blow through the red light before him. Later it was determined the sleepy driver had been traveling for eight straight days and wanted to complete one more delivery before he returned home.

Witnesses at the horrific scene tearfully recalled the small Ford Escort was crushed instantly as the large Kenworth smashed directly into its side. The overwhelming force of the impact halted the speeding momentum of the Kenworth and bounced the crumpled Escort twenty feet away where the crinkled mess looked more devastated than an aluminum coke can that had gone through a compactor.

Standing in front of the gym's main entrance, Malachi pulled his cellphone out of his jean's pocket to see the time. It was now 1:30 and Mom had texted she would be at the school with the report at 1:25. "Doesn't she know that I have to go back to my locker and get my other books and travel all the way across school to get to my history class?" Malachi loved his mother but being a normal teenager, there were times when he found her to be clueless.

# ONE

This was one of those times. His history report was important and if he didn't turn it in on time his grade would slide from an A to a B. Malachi worked hard to keep his grade point average up as he would soon start filling out college applications. It was now 1:35 and again Malachi palmed his cell phone and hastily jammed it back into the stitched enclosure sewed into his jeans. "She has five more minutes and if she doesn't get here, I'm in trouble."

Malachi started texting Karen. "Hurry up, you said you'd be here by now." The messages were never received.

Malachi was not aware that his dad, Mike, was seated in the principal's office leaning forward not able to breathe. At 1:30, Principal James Sowders softly knocked on the wooden door of Mike's classroom, Room #22. Mike was stunned because James seemed to avoid looking at him and Teresa Sykes, another teacher, was with him.

"Mr. Byrge, would you please step into the hallway?" James quietly requested.

"Sure," Mike was taken back by the sad look on Teresa's face.

Mike stepped into the salmon orange painted hallways lined with grey steel lockers and asked James, "What's up? Is something going on?"

"Why don't we go to my office? I have some bad news."

Mike heart started racing. "But what about my class?" Then his head jerked, "Bad news? What kind of bad news?"

"That's why Teresa is here. She can take your class and please, let's go to my office."

Mike's stomach was churning rapidly, "Teresa, we are working on adjectives, it's all on the blackboard."

"Thank you, Mike." And she surprised him as she lunged forward and gave him a comforting embrace.

The walk to James' office seemed to take an eternity and Mike's feet felt like they each weighed 150 pounds and were getting heavier with each step. When they walked by the large counter separating the secretaries from the students, Mike saw the ladies casting sympathetic stares toward him.

"James, what's going on?" Mike said more forcefully than he wanted to.

"Please sit down."

Mike sat down on the burgundy leather chair but did not settle back in a comfortable position. "Mike, I have some bad news. Karen was driving and she was in an accident. She's at the hospital."

"What kind of accident? Was it a fender bender? Was it minor? She's in the hospital? Is she all right?" A plethora of questions shot rapid fire through Mike's mouth.

"Mike, it's bad. You need to find Malachi and get to St. John's Hospital now."

At this time Mike found himself crushed underneath the weight of the news and leaned forward trying to catch his breath. James stepped closer and placed his hand gently on his shoulder, "We are here for you Mike. Whatever you need, let us know."

"Malachi has a free period right now and then will be going to history so he usually goes to the library but he could be anywhere."

"We can page him to the office and he can meet you here."

"Malachi Byrge, please come to the office, Malachi Byrge, please come to the office." Blared the tinny loudspeaker as it echoed throughout the corridors of the school.

When Malachi heard his name, he thought, "Why did Mom take my report to the office? She knew that I was waiting in front of the gym. But then, why do my parents do anything they do?"

Malachi opened the door to the school office and saw his father standing inside the door of the principal's office but his countenance was downcast. Mike raised his hand and motioned him to come. Malachi was bewildered by all the quiet, sad looks he received from those sitting in front of their computers.

Malachi smiled as he walked by the morose secretaries and was trying to figure out why his father seemed so sad. When Malachi walked through the principal's door, Mike pulled him into a tight embrace.

"What's going on?"

"Malachi, Mom has been in an accident and it's bad so we are leaving now and going to the hospital."

"That's not possible. Mom is bringing me my history report and she's just running a little late."

"Have you talked to Mom?"

"We texted about twenty minutes ago."

This information seemed to slightly calm Mike's nerves and he turned toward James, "Thank you for taking care of my class. We're going to go to the hospital now."

James kindly nodded his head in affirmation. "If we can do anything, Mike."

Malachi started telling Mike that he had to stop by his locker to get some books but Mike pressed him. "Right now, let's go to the hospital and see what's going on with your mother. We can come back later and get what we need."

Malachi shrugged his shoulders and started to follow his father who was walking at a faster than normal pace.

Passing through the school was a blur and as they walked out upon the concrete pavement of the teacher's parking lot, Malachi was curious, "Dad, Mom's not hurt, is she? She's O.K., right?"

"Son, I'm not sure what is going on right now and that's why I want to get there quickly."

Mike and Malachi climbed into their blue Dodge Durango and sped out of the parking lot toward the hospital. St. John's Hospital was only ten minutes away but Mike found his heart almost beating out of his chest in nervous anticipation.

Pulling into the hospital parking lot, Mike urged Malachi to hurry up as they exited the Durango. They brushed through the automatic sliding glass doors and briskly approached the circular information desk in the middle of the hallway.

"I'm Mike Byrge and we are looking for my wife, Karen Byrge. She was in an accident. Where can we find her?"

The desk volunteer clad in a pink coat told Mike, "I'm not sure sir, but I will make a call and they will let us know."

Mike sighed a thank you and stepped back from the counter and looked at Malachi. "Mom is going to be all right. She is tough."

A stoic stare overtook the face of the older desk volunteer, "I see. OK, I will tell them," and she slowly hung up the phone.

Looking up sympathetically at Mike, she said, "Sir, do you know where the chapel is in the hospital? There is a room right next to it."

"Yes, I know where the chapel is but what does that have to do with where Karen is at?"

The tightly curled white-haired volunteer spoke with a kind tone, "Sir, the chaplain will meet you in that room."

Malachi stepped up next to Mike. "Dad, why are we talking to the chaplain? How come we can't see Mom?"

In Mike's heart he instinctively knew why they would be talking to a chaplain but all he could come up with was, "I don't know Malachi but let's go." Stepping away from the information counter, Mike remarked to the volunteer, "Thank you."

Malachi was trying to keep up with Mike as it seemed his father was forcing himself in haste toward the chapel. With each step Mike took, his mind reeled, "It can't be, it can't be."

Standing in front of the chapel was a middle aged, bespectacled man wearing a white clerical collar tucked into a black shirt. When they drew near him, the man extended his hand to Mike, "I'm Chaplain Thompson, can we speak in this room?"

Mike reciprocated his handshake and nodded his head. As they walked by the chaplain, he gently placed his hand upon Malachi's shoulder in a reassuring manner. As the three entered the small room, Mike noticed there were four overstuffed, padded chairs with green and pink floral print. On the tables next to them were blue hardcovered Gideon Bibles and color brochures about grief.

Chaplain Thompson asked Mike and Malachi to have a seat and Mike thought how this was the second time today he was asked to have a seat as he awaited news. Malachi settled into the large chair and pushed himself all the way back nesting in. Mike lowered himself and cautiously sat at the edge of the cushioned seat.

"I'm sorry, but I'm afraid I have some terrible news."

Mike took a deep breathe not wanting to admit that he had a terrible feeling about what he was going to hear. The chaplain continued, "Karen, your wife," as he sensitively looked at Mike, "your Mom," turning to Malachi, "died in an automobile accident this afternoon, I'm very sorry."

Mike let out an inhaled breath with a great whoosh as if he had been punched in the stomach by a championship boxer. Malachi tilted his head in shock and reached over and grabbed his father's arm. "What does he mean, Dad? Mom can't be dead. She has to be all right. Right Dad, right?"

Mike shifted toward Malachi and held him in a strong embrace. "Son, she's gone. Mom's dead."

Malachi bristled in the arms of his father. "No, that can't be. She's bringing me my report. Where is she? Is this a joke before my birthday?"

Thick, wet tears were now cascading down Mike's cheeks. "Malachi, it's not a joke."

"It's my fault. If she wouldn't had to bring my report to me, she'd still be alive."

"No, no, no, it was an accident. It is not your fault."

After a long time of holding each other, Mike turned back to the silent chaplain and asked what happened. He supportively explained, "At 1:17 p.m., a large truck broadsided Karen and she died instantly."

Through bloodshot eyes caused by intense grief, Mike asked, "Can we see her? I mean, is it allowed?"

"Of course. Before we go can I have a word of prayer with you?"

Mike agreed but would not hear a word that was said because images of his wife Karen continued to flash in his mind.

Wiping his eyes, Mike stood and pulled Malachi to a standing position embracing him again. The chaplain patiently waited and then led them to the elevator that would take them to the morgue. When they arrived at the large steel door labeled, "Morgue", a technician wearing a white lab coat stepped out and met them.

"We were able to clean her up pretty good but there are still major lacerations and bruises on her face."

Mike was still encased in shock. "How did she die?"

The morgue attendant, attempted to be congenial. "Basically blunt force trauma, her spinal cord was severed and internal organs ruptured."

"Was it quick? Did she suffer?"

The medical professional kindheartedly replied, "Yes, it was instant and she didn't suffer in any manner."

Overtaken with a heartbreak greater than Mike could have imagined, he actually did find some comfort and solace that Karen didn't suffer.

Mike, with more tears flowing down his face turned to Malachi, who was deeply sobbing, "Son, I'm going to go inside and see Mom and then I'll come out and let you know if it is O.K. for you to see her."

Malachi didn't know how to respond, he wanted to see his mom but he didn't want to see her in a lifeless manner.

Mike was escorted through the door by the attendant while the chaplain waited outside in the poorly lit hallway with Malachi. Mike slowly approached the slanted silver autopsy table where the body of his wife rested underneath a white creaseless sheet. The morgue attendant gripped the corners of the sheet and slowly pulled it back revealing Karen's face.

Mike gasped as it just looked like she was sleeping. He did notice several cuts on her forehead and deep bruising on her cheeks. But at any point, she looked like she might open her eyes and say hello. The attendant pointed out that they cleaned her body but did not recommend Mike see the rest of her because of the intense injuries.

Mike agreed and excused himself telling the attendant. "My son needs to say good-bye if he would like. I will be right back."

The attendant solemnly nodded his head.

When the door opened, it seemed to startle Malachi who had been awkwardly standing next to the chaplain. "Mom doesn't look bad. There's some cuts and bruises but if you would like to see her, you can."

Malachi didn't know what he wanted. Yes, he wanted to see her but then no, he didn't. He started slowly shaking his head and gradually started shaking it faster and faster until Mike stepped to him and gathered him in his arms.

Mike assured him it was all right and that they were going to make it but the words were more promises to himself than to his son. The next hour was a blur and eventually they found themselves sitting in their family room where less than a day ago, they were boisterously watching a baseball game.

As they numbly sat speechless on one end of their familiar couch, Malachi broke the cruel silence and said, "Happy Birthday to me." And both he and his father convulsed into gut wrenching mourning.

# *Two*

THE night was going to be long and hard. Both Mike and Malachi pulled a heavy blanket from their beds as they joined each other on the couch in the family room and huddled together. When Mike took hold of the neatly laid out dark green covering, his heart nearly stopped as sad thoughts bombarded him. His hands ran smoothly over the blanket, "Karen was the last one to touch this as she made the bed this morning."

After collecting the blanket, Mike found himself standing at the threshold of he and Karen's room in a daze. Echoes of doubt spiraled through his mind. "She can't be dead. This is just a sick dream. She will come bouncing through that door any minute and wonder why I'm standing here holding our blanket."

But at times, reality can be cruel and it lashed back with a vengeance as Mike wrestled with inner turmoil. "She's not coming back, I'm a single father. This is going to crush Malachi. How are we going to get through this?"

All the frantic activity running rampant in Mike's head was interrupted by Malachi's shaky voice calling out, "Dad, are you all right?"

Mike turned from facing the bedroom, the one he shared with Karen, and responded, "No, son, I'm not all right."

As he was walking down the hallway toward the family room, Mike heard the quiet whimpers of his son as Malachi had looked up at the framed family pictures and found himself reaching out to touch a picture of his mother.

## Two

When Mike saw the tears falling from his son's eyes and his finger trying to touch his mother one last time, he dropped the blanket and rushed to Malachi and pulled him close. Both father and son leaned into each other before they crumpled into a melded heap on the couch.

"Dad, why? It's not fair. She is the best mom." The words were barely audible as Malachi was sobbing so intensely he had to labor to catch his breath.

"Son, I don't know, I hate this, Mom is a Godly woman. She loves God and she helps others and this kind of stuff is not supposed to happen to good people." Mike wasn't sure if he was trying to convince Malachi or himself with this attempt of an explanation.

"But Dad, it's my fault. She had so much to do today and I was a jerk on the phone. That report was so important for my grade but now I don't have her here."

Malachi shook violently. "If I would not have forgot the paper. If I would not have asked her to bring it, she would still be alive."

Mike's heart was not only filled with intense grief because of the loss of his wife but was also broken beyond comprehension. He knew his son was picking up a burden that he would never be able to carry. "Son, it's not your fault. You know your mom. She was always there for anybody who needed help and she loved you so much. She would have been running around today, anyway."

Mike knew his feeble attempt to console Malachi was not successful but there were no courses in college that taught a dad how to help his son with this situation. Mike tenderly tugged Malachi closer so both their hurting hearts would beat together. "Son, let it out, let it out."

The only sound that emanated from their tortured souls were heavy moans accentuated by uncontrollable sobbing. When Malachi was able to catch his breath, he slowly spoke, "What are we going to do Dad? What about school?"

Mike, for a second, seemed to be jolted back to the present, "School, oh yea, I'll call the principal and tell him we're going to take a few days off, he'll understand."

"I don't even want a birthday tomorrow. It won't be the same without Mom."

Mike tried to inject some humor into this impossible time. "Hey, if Mom were here, you know she'd want you to celebrate your birthday. After all, you'll be sweet sixteen and never been kissed."

The inadequate dad joke seemed to elicit a slight chuckle from Malachi. "Dad, you do know I have been kissed, right?"

Mike acted shocked beyond belief and gently pulled away from their tight embrace. "My son, my son! My son has laid his lips on a member of the opposite sex? What is this world coming to?"

Malachi reached up and pulled his waterlogged glasses off of his head. "How are we going to make it without Mom?"

Mike gathered Malachi in for a parting hug. "I don't know. But I do know that she'd want us to figure it out." Then Mike stood and picked his blanket off the floor and pointed to a well-worn spot on the couch, "This is mine."

The night passed slowly as when either father or son managed to slip into a sad slumber, they would awaken each other with low sobbing. The thick padding of the couch caught many tears. Finally, they both succumbed to a physical and much more emotional exhaustion and drifted into a hurting hibernation.

In the morning, Mike was the first to wake up and instinctively looked around and wondered why he was sleeping in the family room. In the midst of a deep grogginess, he also wondered where was Karen and why wasn't she up yet? Then as if a huge weight slammed down upon him, their new normal seized him. Karen is not with us.

Mike collected his blanket into a rumpled pile and slowly walked back to his bedroom and threw the covering upon the bed. To himself, he said, "I'll get that later, I guess from now on, I'll be the one making the bed."

After two more hours, Malachi began stirring. Being a normal teenager, waking up from sleep was a process that could take a while. Sitting up, Malachi was greeted by Mike with the sincerest tone he could produce, "Happy Birthday!"

# Two

Malachi reached out to pick up his glasses from the wooden coffee table. "Yea, it's my birthday today."

"What do you want to eat? Maybe pancakes?" Mike asked as if a delicious breakfast would occupy both their minds instead of the pounding gloom.

"I don't care, Dad. I'm still not hungry," and he started to cry again.

Mike placed the yellow pancake box on the coffee table and once again gathered his son into his arms while wiping the new batch of tears from his own eyes. "We're going to make it, son, I don't know how, but we're going to make it." Mike again trying to comfort himself and his son.

"I hope so, Dad, I do."

The morning hours actually passed quicker than both Mike and Malachi thought they would. "Dad, what do we have to do next? Do we call the church? Do we call a funeral home?"

"I made some calls this morning while you were still sleeping. I called the principal and we can take as long as we want before we go back to school. I also called the church and left a message for Pastor Don and a little later on today, I will call Grisell's funeral home. But for now, let's just hang out." Mike tried to act confidently in front of Malachi but inside, he was just as lost.

After watching the ESPN sports channel and discussing the fate of the Reds, Mike turned to Malachi, "I'm going to lie down now. I don't know if I'll be able to sleep, but I'm going to try."

"Dad, I'm going to hang out on the couch and see if there is anything on tv or any movies on Netflix."

It was 12:42 in the afternoon and as Mike stood, he leaned down and held his son in a clench of comfort. When Mike left the room, Malachi picked up the large, rectangular remote covered by many buttons. If he could only keep his mind off Mom, he would be all right. If only he could find some mind-numbing show to watch, he didn't have to remember what happened yesterday.

During a commercial break, Malachi tiptoed back to his father's room to see how he was doing and was surprised to see him completely entrenched in slumber. Malachi thought, "Good, Dad needs some sleep."

Malachi plopped back onto the couch and nestled in, wrapping the blanket tightly around him when he heard a sound that caused him to perk up. It was his cell phone. But Malachi vaguely remembered turning it off. By now the news of Karen's death was being posted on many Facebook walls and people would flood his phone with short texts of condolences and offers of help. "I thought I turned my phone off. Maybe I didn't."

As Malachi picked up his cellphone, he glanced at the time. It was 1:17 and the number that flashed on the screen said, "Heaven." Malachi's eyes drew closer together in surprise. "Heaven? What is this a joke? How is Heaven calling?"

At first, Malachi almost tossed his phone back on the corner of the coffee table but found himself intrigued so he slid the little green icon of the phone over to the right. "Hello."

"Happy Birthday, my beautiful gift from God," responded the cheerful voice on the other end of the line.

Malachi almost jumped straight up as the voice sounded exactly like his mother. But that was impossible, she was dead. She died from a terrible car accident and now it was only he and his Dad. This must be some form of a malicious and tasteless joke.

Malachi paused as shock filtered through his spirit. "Mom always called me her beautiful gift from God." Malachi remembered he acted like the nickname bothered him when they were with friends and family members but secretly, it made him feel good.

"Who is this?" Malachi tried to manipulate his voice two octaves lower because if this was a prank, it was cruel and he was going to chew them out.

"Malachi, it's me, Mom."

"It can't be. My mother died yesterday in a horrible car accident. Who are you and why are you doing this to me?" Malachi tried to fight back a resurgence of tears.

"Yes, honey, I was in a terrible accident but please know that I'm in Heaven and . . . "

Malachi interrupted his mother or whoever this was on the phone. "Listen, this is not funny. My mom just died last night and I'm going to hang up right now."

"Honey, I know that this seems strange."

"You have one minute because this is weird."

"O.K., ask me any question you want and only questions that you and Dad and I would know."

"All right, what is Dad's middle name?", but then Malachi almost smacked himself on the head because anyone anywhere would have had access to his name and been able to supply it.

"Really, that's all the questions you can think of?"

Malachi's head was swirling with confusion because this was exactly a response his mother would have come back with.

Malachi then regained his composure and thought, maybe I can trick whoever this is on the phone. "All right, I have a question that only my mom and dad would know. How did I get the scar on my right knee?"

"Are you all right? Did something happen just now? You didn't have a scar on your right knee but you do on your left knee. Honey, if something happened, I want to know."

"No, Mom, nothing happened," but then surprised himself that he was calling this unknown caller, "Mom." Malachi continued. "You're right, I don't have a scar on my right knee but how did the one on my left knee happen?"

"Oh, you were about 7 or 8 years old and you cried and cried. You walked into a scrap piece of metal in your uncle's garage and it cut you. When you first rushed into the house with your knee bleeding, you kept screaming, 'I'm suing, I'm suing,' and you had us in stitches."

Malachi became quiet and once again tried to trick the voice on the other end of the line. "Yes, I had to have two stitches."

"No, honey, I remember it was seven stitches because later when we would see your scar, we said that you were seven-up."

"That wasn't funny," Malachi retorted as he was rehearing those words.

"I have another question that only you and dad would know. Where did you hide my Easter basket when I was six years old?" Malachi thought there was no way this person would know this answer. Even though he was much younger, he vividly remembered the Easter basket's hiding place that year and it was the first place he looked every year after that.

"Oh, honey, you were so mad when you couldn't find it. You looked and looked and finally came to us and sighed, 'The Easter bunny must have forgotten about me this year.' Oh, and by the way, we hid it in the dryer behind some of the towels."

Malachi felt his heart racing. "Mom, it is you. But why, I mean how? I mean, I don't know what I mean."

"I know honey, it's a lot to wrap your head around," which was one of Karen's favorite sayings. "It's because it's your birthday today, sweet sixteen. Oh, I wish I could grab you through this phone and just hug you! My baby has turned sixteen years old. Sweet sixteen and never been kissed."

Malachi bristled when he remembered that he was teased by his father the same way. "You and Dad still have the same sense of humor."

"How is Dad? Is he O.K.?"

"Yes, well no, Mom, you're not here. You're dead which I really don't understand how we are talking to each other." Malachi felt himself getting confused.

"I'm so sorry that you two are hurting."

"Of course we are hurting Mom, you died!" And he had to brush back tears.

"I'm so sorry."

Malachi then had an idea. "Dad is laying down because we didn't get much rest last night. Let me go get him so he can talk to you."

"No honey, that's not possible. You'll be the only one who can hear me."

Malachi felt more confused than before. "What do you mean I'm the only one who can hear you?"

*Two*

"The Father granted me an incredible gift. He allowed me to call you on your birthday and only speak to you. If you give your phone to your dad, he won't be able to hear me. Speaking of your phone, when you answered this call you picked it up off the coffee table which, by the way, you guys left an absolute mess with all your drinks and snacks when you were watching the baseball game."

"So, the Father? Are you talking about God?"

Karen's voice became electrified. "Oh yes, honey. God is more real and wonderful and bigger and greater than I could have ever imagined!"

"But you were so close to God when you were alive."

"Yes, but when you see Him in all of His glory, it's breathtaking. Heaven is beautiful. Words can't describe it."

"What is Heaven like? Are there streets of gold and mansions and does God look like an old man with a long white beard?"

"No honey, I can't begin to describe how incredible Heaven is. The light is brighter than you can imagine . . . "

Malachi interrupted her. "Mom, that song, I Can Only Imagine, what did you do when you got there?"

"Honey, one day when you get here, and make sure you GET HERE," she emphasized sweetly, "You will be amazed."

Malachi found himself inundated with so many questions. "Who is there? Tell me about the angels."

Karen seemed to hesitate. "Honey, I can't tell you too much. Our phone calls are a gift from God for me to encourage you and still be your mother."

"What do you mean phone calls? Are we going to get to talk a lot?"

"The incredible gift that God has given us is that I can call you every five years on your birthday at 1:17 p.m."

Malachi winced as he remembered that was the exact time she died so he tried to hide behind humor. "Is that eastern, pacific, or divine time?"

"Honey, I miss your sharp wit already."

"So, let me understand this Mom, you will call me every five years and we can talk?"

"Yes, we can catch up and I'll always be your mother so, I will tell you my opinion."

"I know that you will."

"You will be all right."

Malachi then had a novel question. "Can you see us? I mean does God allow you to watch our lives?"

"Yes, we are allowed glimpses of what is happening in your lives."

"Why only glimpses?"

"Honey, Heaven is a perfect place and there is no pain and no sadness. I can't really describe it because no one who has not been here could comprehend it. We don't see when you are hurting."

"You only see the good times?"

"Yes, God doesn't allow us to see when you're hurting because that would make us sad. But remember, when you are having hard times, you should be looking to God and not at me anyway."

"I really don't get this but this phone call has made my birthday so much better."

"That's the point. The Father knew you were hurting and allowed you this gift."

"I wish we could talk every day! I miss you."

"I know honey, but don't worry, we will talk often. Five years goes very quickly."

Malachi's mind was flooded with queries. "But what do I tell Dad?"

"Tell him to make sure he makes the bed every morning. I'm just teasing. Tell him whatever you would like to. But please know that he may not understand it as this is definitely a unique gift from God."

"How long do we get to talk?"

"As long as the Father allows us to. He knows all things and He knows what's best. Malachi, I want you and your father to know that I love you two with all of my heart."

# Two

Tears slowly started streaming down his cheeks because he often heard that statement from his mother. Choked up Malachi sputtered, "Mom, I'm so sorry you died because you were bringing my report to me. I . . . "

Karen cut him off. "No, no honey, it was an accident. It was not your fault. When it is your time to meet God, you are going to go no matter what is going on. In no way was it your fault and quit thinking like that."

"I know but it's all so weird and new and I don't know what's happening."

"You're right and that is one of the reasons for our phone calls."

"Mom, I love you with all my heart."

Malachi could almost see Karen smiling through the phone as she answered back, "I know honey and I love you. Now I have to say good-bye. I will call you in five years on your birthday at 1:17 p.m. and we'll have so much to catch up on."

"Mom, I love you and I miss you."

"Never forget I love you with all of my heart." And the phone went silent.

For what seemed an eternity, Malachi pressed his phone against his ear and thought, "Could this have happened? Did I really talk to my mom?" Slowly withdrawing it, he quickly pushed the phone button on his screen to see the history of calls received. Malachi was taken back when yes, the last number in his received calls was listed as Heaven but with no corresponding number.

Malachi's heart felt warm as he thanked God for giving him such a wonderful birthday gift. So many things raced through his mind about what was going to happen in the next five years and how he would talk to his mother about them.

Malachi reached out and placed his phone once again on the coffee table and gazed straight ahead. He was shaken back to reality when he saw his father enter the family room.

Mike, still scratching his hair that was tussled after his nap, noticed his son appeared perplexed. "What's going on son? Who were you talking to?"

"Dad, Dad, you are not going to believe this! I was talking to Mom. She called me from Heaven."

"What are you talking about? Talking to Mom?" Mike's face crunched in confusion as he was still waking up.

"Yea Dad and she is in a perfect place where there is no pain and no sadness and she can see us."

"She can see us?"

Malachi's rapid-fire responses bombarded Mike. "Yes, but only the good times because if she saw the bad times, she would be sad."

Mike didn't verbalize what he was thinking but he was concerned that his son was either hallucinating because of grief or making something up.

"Dad, I can tell you are not getting it," then an idea came to Malachi as he navigated to his recent calls, "Look at my last call. It's from Heaven."

Mike took the phone from his son's hands and had to hold it a little distance away as his eyes were still unable to completely focus. "It does say that your last call was from Heaven. But was it a telemarketer? Was it someone trying to play a joke?

Malachi found himself getting a little frustrated. "Dad, no, it was Mom! She is going to call me every five years on my birthday at 1:17."

"Son, you know that's the exact time Mom died."

"Yes, but she's good, Dad. She's with God."

Mike, still not believing his son, said, "Son, if thinking that Mom has called you makes you feel better I'm happy for you."

"Dad, that's all right if you don't understand it. I really don't understand it either but it is the best birthday gift that I've ever had."

Mike playfully swatted toward his son. "Better than any gift that I have ever given you?"

"Yes, Dad, it was Mom."

Days later, Malachi continually went over every word that he and Karen exchanged. He still felt an overwhelming sadness but when the heaviness came over him, he remembered their conversation. "If only Dad believed me, he would feel a little better."

It was the morning before the funeral service and it seemed so much had transpired in the last few days. Mike and Malachi returned to the school and picked up assignments he had missed. They also met with Connie and Elliot Grisell at the funeral home where the Grisell family had been serving the community for eighty years.

As Malachi walked through the light blue carpeted hallway, he glanced at the historical mementos tucked back in the glass enclosed shelves. It hit him that he had only attended two other funerals and they were both older relatives that he did not know very well. Connie and Elliot warmly invited Mike and Malachi into the tranquil arrangement room to discuss the details of Karen's service.

After that, Mike and Malachi went to Kroger to pick up much needed supplies. As they were wandering through the multi-shelved aisles of bread and soda pop and spaghetti sauce, Mike sadly remembered that grocery shopping was on Karen's final list of things. Of course, Mike and Malachi bought more junk food than Karen would have allowed, but now it was just the boys.

Three days later, the funeral began at 2:00 p.m. and Malachi felt a strange peace come over him. Earlier, during the long-lined visitation, countless people, relatives, friends, and others that Malachi had never seen before, mobbed him in numerous embraces. They all were saying how wonderful Karen was and how much she will be missed.

At this point in the service, Pastor Don was quoting Psalm 23 and explaining how King David had a close, personal relationship with the Lord and that we could as well. Malachi smiled to himself when the pastor arrived at verse 6, "And I will dwell in the house of the Lord forever," because he pictured his mother with God.

Mike chose to share a few memories of his wife and spoke eloquently even though there were times he had to fight back tears. He sweetly recounted stories of joy and overcoming challenges together. Near the end of his well-crafted eulogy, Mike looked straight at Malachi and said, "And your mother loved you with all of her heart."

Happiness welled within Malachi because of this comment but he wanted to stand up and publicly announce, "I know that my mother loved me with all of her heart because she called me from Heaven." But he decided not to because people might have thought he had cracked under the pressure of grief.

After the service at the ornately decorated funeral home, mourners remarked to Malachi and each other how he seemed to be doing all right. When a well-wisher would make this comment to Malachi, he replied, "I know that my mom is in Heaven and it is a perfect place and she's happy."

Some people politely shook their heads in agreement with his reply while others were taken back and almost perceived it as being glib. But Malachi knew what he knew. He had talked to his mother and she was with God.

As the sad entourage walked over the grassy areas in the cemetery, making sure to avoid stepping on the weathered concrete headstones, they closed in together near the plot where Karen's body would be lowered into the ground. Malachi took it all in as he saw the overturned dirt by the side of the opening of earth now with his mother's casket hovering over it.

Malachi didn't remember and couldn't repeat many of the comments or stories shared at Karen's service but the words in the final prayer, "Ashes to ashes, dust to dust," reverberated through his heart.

Again, he wanted to loudly proclaim. "My mom is not dead. She is more alive than she ever was. She is in Heaven and waiting for us. I know this for a fact because I talked to her on the phone on my birthday." But he didn't.

# *Three*

T HE whirlwind of emotions of the funeral died down and now
Mike and Malachi were adjusting to their new normal. As
Mike walked back through the noisy, crowded school hallways, he
was kindly consoled and hugged by friendly coworkers. Many of
Malachi's friends sought him out but were not quite sure what to
say. Dealing with grief for teenagers is challenging because many
don't experience it until much later in life.

It was Malachi's junior year and when Karen was alive there
had been numerous conversations about where he was going to
go to college and what he was going to study. Now Malachi was
more introspective and knew he didn't have to rush into making a
decision right away.

When Mike brought up the topic of graduation, he did so
tactfully and didn't want to push or discourage Malachi. They were
slowly settling into a routine and a stock statement soon fell from
both of their lips, "If Mom were here, you would not be getting
away with that." It was a mutual observance of how much they
both missed Karen.

There were times when Malachi found himself gripped by
grief and all of a sudden just started to get choked up. During
those times, he always flashed back to the phone call from Heaven
and even though he was still deeply mourning, it did make him
feel a little better. But Malachi was deeply worried about his father.

Mike was trying to keep it all together to boost his son's mo-
rale but there were times when he had to abruptly turn away and

walk into another room. There were times when sadness overtook him midsentence and later he would come back to Malachi and apologize asking, "What was I saying?"

Malachi felt his junior year of school passed quickly. He had played on the basketball team and as a starter, he was able to compete on the court a lot but he knew that this would not be a pursuit after high school. He also played the drums for the school band and enjoyed the camaraderie and friendships he developed.

Whenever Malachi was breaking loose on a galloping fast break toward the opponent's basket or pounding out the rhythm for the marching band, he always looked up and saw Mike sitting on the uncomfortable metal rows of the bleachers watching with a smile.

After one of the band concerts, as Mike and Malachi were walking into their house, Mike stopped and gazed at Malachi, "Son, you know that your mother would be so proud of you."

Malachi leaned towards his father who he now matched his height. "Thanks Dad and I know."

A plethora of emotions ran through Malachi's heart as his 17th birthday drew near. "Maybe Mom will call this year too." Then there were times when fearful doubts loomed, "Maybe God changed the rules and she won't call me anymore." Whenever he went back and forth about the future of the phone calls, he found that he missed his mother much, much more.

Malachi's senior year passed as a blur too. Before he and Mike realized it, Malachi was striding across an elevated stage wearing a blue flowing gown and a squared hat with a gold tassel tangling from it as he received his diploma. Mike continually hugged his son and reminded him how much his mother loved him.

Malachi had a stock reply when his father shared something heartfelt about Karen. "Dad, I know, we talked on the phone when I turned sixteen, remember?"

"Oh yea, I forgot about that."

Malachi was not sure if his dad really believed that his mother called him that day. The day after Malachi's 18th birthday during his senior year, Mike asked him, "Did you get a call from your mother?"

Malachi knew that he wasn't trying to be malicious but it came off that way. "Dad, I told you, we are only going to talk every five years."

At that response, Mike stood there not quite sure what to say. Malachi was now going to take another step on his young adult journey and venture to college. Mike's heart burst with joy when Malachi told him, "I've decided to go to Ball State University and study history. I want to be a teacher."

Ball State University is in Muncie, Indiana about twenty miles away from Anderson. Malachi had chosen to live at home and commute to save some money as he would not have to pay to live in a dorm. Plus, it allowed him to stay and help his dad. There were times when Mike seemed befuddled as he terribly missed Karen.

Malachi's first two collegiate years seemed to fly by as he took a variety of courses to fulfill the required general education classes that all students had to muddle through. He immensely enjoyed the beginning history ones and was looking forward to digging much deeper into his studies during his last two years.

Mike and Malachi intentionally scheduled time together usually incorporating a Reds game where they both let loose. Mike was stunned how his son was growing so quickly and could not believe that soon he would be 21 years old.

"What would you like to do on your 21st birthday?"

Malachi conjured a mocking look on his face. "Why would I want to spend my 21st birthday with my Dad?" And they both laughed.

Mike hesitantly broached a subject that he had purposely been quiet about the last couple of years, "Son, do you think your mother will call you this birthday?"

Malachi had noticed that his dad had not talked about the phone call in the last two years, "I hope so. Five years ago, she said she would. But you never know. Either way, I still miss Mom. It would be nice to hear her voice."

"Yes, it would."

The day of Malachi's birthday he had classes all day and he and Mike had arranged to meet in the evening and go out to eat at Malachi's favorite restaurant, Texas Roadhouse. Over a thick, juicy steak, Malachi, a surprise visitor, and his dad would enjoy each other's company.

The morning classes passed tediously with each minute seeming to last an eternity. Malachi had to remind himself over and over again, "Quit looking at the clock. Quit looking at the clock!" But he couldn't help himself and soon, he was calculating how much time before the professor would free them from the never-ending lecture.

Malachi did have an afternoon class at 1:00 and it was one he liked. He enjoyed learning about ancient civilizations like the Mesopotamians and Babylonians and how their world impacted our world today. But Malachi knew today he could not sit still at a brown, wooden desk and pay attention to a droning professor standing in front of a large white board covered with historic dates.

Near the student center was a small, flower filled patio area where a few students retreated to a space of solace. Malachi decided he would have privacy there and also the serene scene reminded him of his mother. Racing thoughts continued to assail him. "Would Mom call? What if I imagined it five years ago? What if God doesn't think I should have this gift anymore?"

Malachi's consuming worries and negative assaults were interrupted by the ringing of his phone. It was 1:17 p.m. Not quite trembling, but not steady, Malachi's hand raised his phone so he could see the caller id imprinted upon its screen and it read, "Heaven".

Joy spread across Malachi's face as he fought back tears when he heard a familiar greeting, "Happy Birthday, my beautiful gift from God!"

"Mom, it's you!"

"Yes, honey, I told you I'd call you every five years, I can't believe how quick it has gone."

"Yes, Mom, I know that you said you would call every five years but I didn't know if God changed His mind or if maybe the rules had changed."

"Honey, when the Father makes a promise, He always keeps it."

Malachi had so many questions running through his mind. "Is Heaven still great? I mean what do you do all day? Do you stand around and worship all day?"

"Yes, Heaven is still perfect and it is incredible. There is constant worship and it is the sweetest experience but we are not here just sitting on fluffy clouds listening to winged angels strum stringed harps."

"Mom, I have a question. What do the angels look like?" As the last five years passed, Malachi found himself drifting away as he tried to process abstract thoughts about Heaven.

"I'm going to try to explain it in a way that people on earth could understand. Angels are spirit beings and you can see them but they're fluid."

"Fluid? I'm not sure what that means."

"I know honey, it's so hard to explain Heaven."

"Are you a spirit being too?"

"No, honey, when you come to Heaven, the Father gives you a new body. Remember the Bible talks about an imperishable, immortal, incorruptible body?"

Maybe because Malachi was now in college and his professors were pushing him to think critically, he wasn't quite satisfied with his mother's answers. "Mom, I'm not really getting what you are telling me."

"That's all right. There is nothing wrong with not understanding Heaven. Just know this, it is more beautiful and peaceful and joyful than you could imagine."

"Dad and I have talked about you in Heaven and I think it makes him feel better knowing you're there."

"How is Dad?" Karen quietly asked.

"He's doing much better. The first couple of years after you died . . . "

Karen interrupted him. "Honey, yes, the shell that I was in on earth died, but I really didn't die, I came to Heaven."

"Yes, Mom, the first couple years after you went to Heaven was really hard on Dad. He even had a hard time going to church."

"He didn't stop going, did he?"

"No, Pastor Don was very helpful and spent a lot of time with Dad and that was really good."

"Please tell him that I miss him."

"I definitely will but I'm not sure he believes you called the first time when I turned 16."

"I know, but did the phone call help you?"

"It helped more than you know Mom. When everyone was sad, I knew that you were good and in a perfect place. It really helped."

"Good, that's why we can talk every five years. So, tell me, how was the last couple years of high school? Tell me everything!"

"Mom, high school was so long ago. I'm almost done with college."

"I know, you're a young man now."

"High school was good, we missed you at all the events. Dad didn't miss any of my basketball games and was always watching when I played the drums."

Malachi could tell his mother was smiling. "I know that he was there for you. He loves you so much."

"But Mom, I do have to let you know that we missed you terribly. I even caught myself looking up in the stands and wondering why you weren't sitting next to Dad."

"I know honey. Do you remember the time when Dad was upset that the referee didn't call a foul on the other player when he intentionally pushed you and Dad was really loud?"

Malachi snickered. "I know, we thought he was going to get kicked out of the gym. You were so mad at him that you didn't talk to him on the ride home. It sure was an awkward ride."

"Yes, it was. But that was the last time, he yelled at the refs, wasn't it?"

"Mom, when you put your foot down, we knew you were serious."

"What about your friends from high school? What are they doing?"

Malachi ventured into his memory banks trying to remember which of his friends that Karen would have known. "They are doing good. Remember Anna? She went to nursing school right after graduation and will be starting soon in a hospital in Indianapolis."

"That's nice, I remember you two had classes together since you were little. Was it in second grade she gave you a Valentine's Day card and you were upset because you thought it meant that you two were married?"

"No, it was the third grade and I was not upset."

"Malachi Edward, remember I was there."

"Maybe it was a little weird but we've always been friends."

"What about Kenny and the other friend? What was his name, David? You always spent a lot of time together."

"Kenny is here with me at college and David went to a trade school and became certified as a welder."

"That's nice, you boys had good times."

"Yea but it's good that you and Dad didn't know everything we did."

"Don't be too sure. Dad and I knew more than you think we knew. So how is college, how are your classes, do you like it?"

"Mom, I love college. I love my classes, it's so cool to be studying history."

"You've always liked history. Were there any classes that you didn't like?"

Malachi shook his head as he remembered with disdain. "I didn't like the prerequisite math classes I had to take. You remember how much I struggled with math."

Karen remembered the many late-night study sessions of math and how frustrated Malachi would become. "I can recall sitting around our dining room table many nights trying to go over fractions and later algebra."

"Well, it didn't get any easier for me but now those classes are done so I can focus on the ones for my major."

"So what are you going to be?" Karen knew the answer but wanted to hear it from Malachi.

"You are joking right? You know that I am studying history and am going to be a teacher."

"That is wonderful! Are you living in a dorm on campus?"

At this time, Malachi found himself a little confused. "Mom, I thought you were able to see us?"

"Yes, we can, except when you are hurting or sad."

"So you know what I'm doing, that I'm living at home and you should even know what I'm studying, so why are you asking?"

Malachi was not trying to be rude but was trying to form some sort of order out of how the phone calls worked.

"You're right. I do know many of the answers to the questions I'm asking you but it's good to hear you answer them. And yes, the Father allows us to see you during the good times but we don't see everything."

"Mom, the more you explain, the more I don't understand."

"I know honey, but one day it will all make sense."

Then another question popped into Malachi's mind. "But Mom, what if I tell you something sad on the phone when we're talking? Won't that contradict Heaven? I mean if it's a perfect place with no pain and I mention something bad, won't you be sad?"

"Honey, the Father and I talked about that and if I'm ever sad because of something that has been brought up in our conversation, the Father allows me to see deeper."

"What do you mean, deeper?"

Karen was trying to put it into words that Malachi would understand. "O.K., you know that the Father is always working, right?"

"Yes."

"He is always working things out for the best of those who love Him so even during hard and sad times, the Father is providing or growing you for something else. The Father told me that if you share anything sad in our conversations He will allow me to see how He'll use those tough times for your good."

"Wow, I really don't get it but in a weird way, it makes sense and makes me feel good."

"Good, that's what the phone calls are supposed to do. So, tell me everything, have you met anyone special?"

"What do you mean, Mom?"

"You know what I mean young man. Have you met a young lady yet?'

"Mom, I know lots of young ladies."

"Malachi, you know what I mean. Are you seeing anyone?"

Malachi enjoyed the cat and mouse game he was playing with his mother. "Mom, I see a lot of people when I am on campus."

"Malachi Edward!"

"That's the second time you've called me Malachi Edward."

"Give me the scoop. What do you young people say, 'Give me the 411?'"

"Mom, no one has said that for many years."

"So, is there a young lady in your life?"

"Yes, Mom, I am dating someone."

"Well, tell me about her. What's her name? Where's she from? Has Dad met her? How serious is it?"

Malachi's head was spinning at the barrage of inquiries. "Whoa, slow down Mom. Her name is Lisa and she's not from Indiana. She's actually from Wheeling, West Virginia."

"A mountaineer, huh?"

"Yes, a mountaineer, and no Dad has not met her yet, but he will tonight."

"I have a question and this may be a little awkward for you to hear but is your dad dating at all?"

"Mom, you're right that was awkward. I mean that would be really hard if Dad were dating someone. Wouldn't it hurt you?"

"Honey, no, I love your father and always will but I want him to be happy too. He is still young and maybe one day will find someone to fall in love with."

Malachi really had not thought a great deal about his father having another relationship. "Do you really mean that? I mean wouldn't you feel like he replaced you?"

"Honey, your father and I had a special relationship and we'll always love each other but God's plan was for me to come to Heaven quicker than we thought. I always want him to be happy."

"So tonight when I see Dad should I tell him that Mom wants him to start dating?"

"Very funny, young man, I just want your dad to be happy. Enough dodging, tell me more about Lisa."

Malachi slowly started to describe Lisa but then found himself speaking faster. "Mom, you would love her. She's beautiful. She has blonde hair and she's funny. You're not going to believe this, but she played basketball in high school too."

"Really? Now you're going to tell me that she played drums too."

"Very funny, Mom, no, she did not play the drums," Malachi continued, "but she did play the flute."

"You two do have a lot in common. How did you meet her?"

"That's a fun story. We had a math class last year . . . "

"Math? Are you consorting with math people?"

"Yes, she's really good at math."

"Oh, I see, that's how you made it through your math classes without me."

"Absolutely, I had to find a late-night study partner since you're in Heaven."

"I hope there were not too many late nights and they were not very late."

"Mom, don't worry, she is a good girl and we pray together and she goes to church."

"Honey, that's the greatest thing. When you find a Christian partner, it makes marriage a lot easier."

"I know that you and Dad had a great marriage."

"We did. There were rough times every now and then so I had to straighten him out."

"I remember."

"So, she's beautiful. She played sports in high school. She's good at math. Have you met her parents?"

"I knew that you would get around to that question! I haven't met her parents yet but next month is our spring break and we're going to visit her family."

"Wow, that's a big step. Is this the one?"

"Mom, I think she might be. I'm really thinking about asking her to marry me next year and maybe right after college getting married."

"Honey, that is wonderful. You said that Dad hasn't met her yet but does he know about possible plans of marriage?"

"He doesn't know yet but we've talked a lot about her. He keeps hinting that I should propose to her but he always says it in a goofy manner, you know Dad."

"Yes, I do know your father. His humor was one of the first things that attracted me to him. We don't have too much more time but do you have any plans for your birthday?"

Malachi felt jarred back into the reality that the phone call wouldn't last forever. "That's right, I wish we could talk forever."

"Me too, honey."

After a brief interlude of sadness knowing their phone call would soon be over and he wouldn't be able to talk to his mother for another five years, Malachi said, "You asked about plans, yes, Dad and I are going to Texas Roadhouse tonight."

"Is Lisa going too?"

"She might be going. Of course, she's coming but Dad doesn't know yet so I'm afraid he might tell some of his dad jokes."

In almost a sad tone, Karen quietly said, "I miss those dad jokes."

Then, almost as if a switchboard operator indicated that time was up, she said, "Honey, we have to say good-bye for another five years but I have enjoyed talking to you so much. Please tell your father that I love him and if Lisa is the one, I'm so happy for you."

"Mom, I love talking with you but I hate this part of having to say good-bye."

"I know, Malachi, I love you."

"Mom, I love you too," Malachi found himself fighting to hold back tears.

"I will call you in another five years and am looking forward to hearing you."

"Mom, it will go fast," Malachi was not sure if he was trying to convince himself or her

"I know it will honey," Karen's voice was trailing off, "Never forget that I love you with all of my heart." And the phone went silent.

Malachi sat in the stillness of the shade of the flower filled area for a short time. He was so thankful that he'd been able to talk to his mother but it also reminded him how much he missed her. A rhetorical question rummaged around in Malachi's mind if he was better off not being able to talk to Karen. But as the wind softly blew through the stretching lilies and gorgeous tulips releasing their fragrant aroma, Malachi knew that like the pleasant smell he was enjoying, the calls from his mother were pleasing as well.

Leaving the student center, Malachi walked to the three-story library to connect with Lisa at four thirty to drive to Anderson to meet Mike so they could revel in a birthday dinner celebration.

When Malachi arrived, the library had been bustling as many students scurried through the book covered shelves trying to retrieve the ones they needed. Sitting at a long, brown, wooden table in an uncomfortable straight back wooden chair, Malachi passed the time poring over notes he had scribbled down in his earlier classes.

After the first phone call from Heaven, Malachi later thought about each word and each inflection of his mother's voice. This call was no different and he found himself laughing audibly when he remembered some of their comments to each other.

Malachi's thoughts were jarred when he heard, "Hi honey." For a brief second, his mind flashed back to Karen but when he looked up he saw the smiling visage of his girlfriend, Lisa.

"You look like you have a lot of things on your mind, birthday boy."

THREE

Malachi rose and embraced her. "I was just thinking that I haven't had a birthday kiss yet."

"You better not have had a birthday kiss yet, mister."

After they pressed their lips gently together, Lisa softly said, "Happy Birthday."

Malachi again leaned forward for another kiss. "Yes, and if I can get another kiss it will be a happier birthday."

Lisa succumbed to his desired advance and then Malachi turned and scooped up his notebooks placing them back into his red and gray backpack. Extending his right hand to Lisa and closing it around her grip as she held his, they exited the library and started walking out to the student parking lot where Malachi's used light blue Toyota Camry was parked.

Malachi gripped the handle of the passenger door and opened it for Lisa and she turned to him. "Thank you kind sir."

Bowing with a grandiose gesture, Malachi walked around the car to the driver's side, opened the door, threw his supply filled backpack in the rear seat and settled into the driver's seat. Looking over at Lisa, his face took on a serious countenance.

Malachi's solemn appearance shocked her a little. "Is everything all right? You look very serious right now."

As he turned the ignition key to the starting position and the engine roared to life, Malachi responded to her, "Lisa, there's something I've never shared with you and don't worry it's not bad but it's kind of strange."

"What is it?"

Malachi decided not to drive yet but wanted to tell Lisa about the phone calls from Heaven but was not quite sure how to start. He knew that if he blurted out that he had just spoken with his dead mother and that she calls from Heaven every five years that might cause Lisa to wonder if he needed psychiatric help.

"Lisa, you know my mom died five years ago."

Lisa reached over with her left hand placing it upon Malachi's shoulder in a comforting manner. "Yes, honey, you told me."

"Well I didn't tell you everything."

"Whatever it is, you can tell me."

"Lisa, Mom died a day before my sixteenth birthday and the Father gave me and her a special gift."

"Yes, you said she knew the Lord so God gave her eternal life in Heaven, right?"

Malachi slowly nodded his head. "Yes, and God gave us another gift. She called me the day after she died. It was on my 16th birthday and she calls every five years on my birthday."

"But today is your birthday and it was five years ago that you were sixteen so are you saying you got a call from your dead mother today?"

Malachi gently squeezed her hand. "That's right. And by the way, Mom is not dead, she is in Heaven. She's more alive than she's ever been."

"I really don't understand."

"That makes two of us who don't understand. As we're going to meet Dad, I'll explain it to you."

Lisa still not sure what her boyfriend was saying, tugged her seatbelt clicking it into place and turned back to Malachi. "This will be an interesting conversation."

"More than you know."

# *Four*

M ALACHI reached down, gripped the black leather covered gear shift, and slowly moved it into reverse. Glancing backwards, he saw Lisa out of his peripheral vision and noticed that the thoughts inside her head were whirling. Malachi smoothly placed the car into drive to move forward out of the school parking lot. After he turned to look out the windshield, he quipped, "You O.K.?"

Lisa, whose gaze seemed transfixed to an unknown point in front of her responded, "Sure, I'm great. My boyfriend just told me he talks to, not his dead mother, but his mother who went to Heaven five years ago."

"Yes, it's strange but it's kind of cool too, don't you think?"

"Yes, it's definitely great, but why you?"

"That's an incredible question. Mom told me it was because I was sad and the Father wanted to give me a birthday gift."

"The Father, do you mean God?" Lisa found a multitude of questions flying around in her mind.

"Yes, that's what Mom calls Him."

"But many mothers have died and how many sons miss them so why don't all of them get calls?"

Malachi's eyes squinted a little bit, not because of the sun affecting his vision, but because he'd not really thought of that particular question. "I don't know, that's a great question. Yea, I don't have any idea but I'm really glad it's happening."

"Your mother calls on your birthday, how do you know when she will call?"

Malachi laughed but then caught himself when he realized that Lisa was not joining in. "I know when she's going to call because it's at the same time every five years, 1:17 p.m. . . . . "

"But isn't that when your mother died?"

"Honey, you have a good memory. Remind me not to ever do anything wrong."

"That's right mister. In the Bible it says hell has no fury like a woman's scorn."

"I'm not sure if that is in the Bible."

Lisa spoke authoritatively, "If it's not, it should be. Now stop trying to change the subject. So, your mom calls every five years on your birthday at exactly 1:17 p.m.? How long do you get to talk? What does she say?"

"We talk as long as God allows but I always wish we could talk longer. We talk about all kinds of things and she slips in motherly advice," and as Malachi said, "motherly advice", he raised his right hand and made quotation marks in the air.

Slight wrinkles were creasing in Lisa's forehead which happened when she was confused about something and Malachi thought that made her appear even cuter than normal. "Does your Dad talk to your mom? Does he know about the phone calls?"

"No, Dad wouldn't be able to hear her and you won't be able to either but he does know about the calls."

"How does he know and what does he think about them?"

"I told him right after the first phone call and he thinks about them like you're thinking about them. You're not sure."

"I'm definitely sure that I'm not sure about it. Speaking of your Dad, does he know that I'm coming to your birthday dinner?"

"I might have forgotten to tell him that you were coming."

Lisa briskly pulled her hand from Malachi's grip. "Malachi Edward!"

Malachi thought to himself. "Before Mom went to Heaven, she used my first and middle name and now she uses them every five years but here my future wife is using it. Oh my."

"Isn't your dad going to be surprised that you walk in with a girl?"

"No, it happens all the time."

Lisa moved back against the passenger door. "What? Did you just say you take girls out to eat with your father all the time?"

"Maybe I did, but I've never brought a beautiful woman that I'm madly in love with and want to spend the rest of my life with to him before."

Lisa forced herself not to smile as she twisted her body to glance straight ahead. "You were almost in a lot of trouble."

"I love you," Malachi reached over and tenderly gripped her hand.

Lisa could not help for a smile to break through on her face this time. "I love you too."

As they exited off of I-69 and turned right on Scatterfield Road entering Anderson, Malachi thought briefly that this may have been the turn the trucker took before taking his mother's life. Lisa seemed to sense Malachi was falling back into a hurtful memory so she took her right index finger and affectionately massaged the back of Malachi's hand that was holding hers.

Malachi perked up. "Almost here, we'll turn left then we'll be there."

Lisa did want one more question answered before she met his father, "You have told him that we were dating, right?"

"Sure! Maybe? No, I'm pretty sure I told him about us." Then he settled into a parking spot just left of the double swinging door entrance of the busy restaurant of Texas Roadhouse.

Lisa cast him a phony menacing look as she unbuckled her seat belt and proclaimed, "I'm opening my own door because of that comment."

"As you wish," quoting the movie, The Princess Bride, one that he and Lisa loved watching together.

As Malachi stepped out of the car he surveyed the parking lot, crowded with oversized trucks and sturdy jeeps, and noticed his father's car. "He's here. His car is over there."

Meeting together in the front of the car, Lisa gazed intently into Malachi's eyes. "Honey, I really wish you would've told me that he didn't know I was coming. I would've worn a different outfit."

"He is going to love you, no matter how you are dressed." And their lips tenderly made contact.

"Remember, my dad is goofy and can make some dumb jokes."

Hand in hand, they walked into the western style entrance of Texas Roadhouse and were immediately greeted in a friendly fashion with a high pitched, fake Texas accent, "Howdy, welcome to Texas Roadhouse! How many?" Her voice was almost drowned out by the blaring country songs reverberating through the loud, grainy restaurant jukebox.

Malachi answered the blue jean, green plaid shirt wearing young hostess, "We're meeting my father here and he probably already has a table."

The perky, long brown braided haired young lady said with a smile, "Then follow me," as she plucked a couple of oversized menus out of a wooden holder and retrieved a couple of pairs of silverware tightly wrapped in a black cloth napkin. Stepping toward the seating area, Malachi beheld the nice choice cuts of sirloin behind the glass window and squeezed Lisa's hand as they heard the crunching noises of discarded, broken peanut shells being trampled underneath their feet.

As this little entourage paraded toward a table with one lone diner, Lisa quickly noticed how much Malachi resembled his father. Mike had been studying the plastic covered oversized menu as they approached but when he saw Lisa, he rose to his feet and exclaimed, "I'm sorry, I'm here to have a birthday dinner with my son and I had no idea he was going to bring the most beautiful college student at Ball State with him."

Lisa mildly blushed as Malachi whispered to her, "I told you he was goofy."

Lisa slid across the orange padded seat toward the wall as Malachi sided up next to her. Mike sat back down and looked at

FOUR

Malachi. "Happy Birthday, 21 years old. Wow, I just can't believe it."

"Thanks Dad and by the way, this is Lisa."

Mike smiled which made Lisa feel at ease. "Lisa, I'm very glad to meet you. Tell me about yourself. Are you and Malachi going to get married?"

Malachi frowned. "Dad! Lisa, I told you to be aware of his dad jokes."

A toothy smile erupted upon Lisa's face. "Honey, don't worry, my dad tells some of the corniest jokes there are. I'm used to them."

"Corny jokes, ha Dad, Lisa has known you less than two minutes and is already onto you."

"So you are." A friendly grin spread across Mike's face.

For the next two hours, they joked and teased and needled and laughed together. They might have occupied and stayed in the booth next to decorative Texas memorabilia hanging on the wall longer but they noticed the small crowd by the door waiting to be seated.

After writing his signature upon the bill encased in the black elongated folder, Mike looked at Lisa, "I'm really glad you came and that I was able to meet you."

"Thank you. I had a great time and your son means a lot to me."

Mike fondly looked over at Malachi. "He means a lot to me and his mother too." Even after five years of being gone, Mike often referred to Karen when he responded.

As he pushed up out of his seat, Malachi clutched Lisa's hand as she scooted across the padded bench they had sat on for the last couple of hours. "Dad, we'll see you soon."

Mike never missed an opportunity to be mischievous. "We, does that mean that I get to see Lisa again?"

"Yes, does that we mean, you and Lisa?" Lisa asked as her head swiveled toward Malachi.

"Of course it does, please don't let this guy's humor rub off on you."

"Come here son, Happy Birthday. It used to be sweet sixteen and never been kissed so I guess now it's 21 and still never been kissed."

Malachi scrunched his face up in mock disdain and Lisa replied in a spirited manner, "Oh, he's been kissed."

It was now Malachi's turn to gawk at Lisa as his eyes opened widely.

Mike loudly roared. "My son, my son. Carousing with women. Where have I gone wrong?"

Malachi placed his arm around Lisa. "You didn't do anything wrong Dad, you and Mom taught me what true love was and I've found mine."

The awkwardness was accentuated by the sweet reply as Lisa nestled closer to Malachi and Mike warmly said, "Son, I love you and I'm proud of you."

During the next five years, many major events transpired. Malachi and Lisa graduated college and were married. They both started working and five years later when Karen calls Malachi has much news to share.

It was a Saturday when Malachi turned 26 years old. He and Lisa talked about how he needed to be alone at 1:17 p.m. She honored his wishes and arranged to spend some time with a former college roommate at a local Starbucks restaurant, sipping coffee, and reminiscing about the fun times they had at Elliot Hall.

At the prearranged time of 1:17, Malachi's phone rang, the word Heaven flashed across the top of his screen and he heard words that made his heart jump. "Happy Birthday, my beautiful gift from God!"

"Mom, it is so good to hear your voice!"

"Honey, I love hearing your voice too."

"Mom, so much has happened since we last talked. Even though it has only been five years, it seems like it has been a lifetime."

"Tell me everything. I want to know every detail. The last time we talked you were still in college and I seem to recall that you were spending time with a young lady."

Malachi almost blushed by the saccharinely sweet tone his mother took. "Well, we're more than spending time together. Lisa and I got married and have been married for almost three years now."

"I knew it. How is she? How are you two doing? Wait, go back, I want to hear about college too."

Malachi felt his head was spinning as so much had transpired since their last talk. "School was wonderful Mom. Lisa and I graduated together. I finally finished all my required history classes and wrote my exit thesis."

"What was your thesis about?"

"Significant battles of the Civil War."

"You have always loved writing about the battles, even in high school."

Malachi felt a small tinge of guilt when he remembered the report his mother was bringing to him when she was killed was about a Civil War battlefield so all he could muster was, "Yea."

Karen didn't stop her pursuit of questions. "So how was graduation? How did you feel when you received your degree?"

"It was wonderful Mom. We really missed you. When I walked across the stage, Dad stood up and yelled, 'That's my boy'. It was almost embarrassing but it was really cool."

"Your Dad. What a character. What about Lisa? What was her degree?"

"Mom, you know the answer to all these questions. I thought you saw glimpses of us?"

"I did but I love hearing it from you. It makes me feel like I was there when you talk about it."

"Mom, I will be honest, it was hard not having you there but I know that you're in a perfect place. But please know that you're still missed."

"Enough about me. Tell me about Lisa! You didn't tell me her degree and now you're married. Tell me how you proposed!"

Malachi grinned as he was caught up in the enthusiasm of his mother's curiosity. "She graduated with a degree in accounting, just like someone else I know. Now the proposal was another story."

"Don't you dare leave a word out about it, tell me."

"Mom, it was great. We went out to dinner . . . "

"Where?"

"Slow down Mom, I will get there," Malachi playfully chided her. "We went to Applebee's and had a nice dinner and then we drove out to Edgewater Park . . . "

"Oh I loved that place, once your father and I . . . "

"Mom, I am never going to get to tell you everything if you keep interrupting me."

"I know, I know. I just love talking to you."

"I love talking to you too Mom. At Edgewater Park, we hiked for a little bit and then sat down on an old, weathered picnic table and I asked her if she would marry me."

"You did get down upon one knee, didn't you? Did you wait for her to say yes?"

A grin spread across Malachi's face as he felt he was nine years old again and his mom was asking if he had washed his face and brushed his teeth before bed. "Yes, Mother, I did all those things. And yes, she did say yes."

"What did your Dad think? The last time we talked he hadn't met her yet."

"Dad loves Lisa. He liked her the first time they met at Texas Roadhouse and we've done a lot of things together. I think there may be times when he enjoys hanging out with her as much as with me."

"I'm sure that's not true. Your father has always loved you."

"Mom, I know, I was just teasing."

"So, when did you propose and when did you get married?"

"Oh Mom, I'm not sure, it was all a blur. I'm just kidding. I proposed in the middle of our last year of college and we were married a year after graduation."

"So after graduation, you were engaged for a year, what did you two do?"

Malachi wondered if his mother was checking up to see if they had behaved themselves. "Mom, if you were wondering if we lived together, we didn't. After graduation, I stayed with Dad and Lisa got an apartment over on 60th street."

"I remember those apartments. They were just building them right before I came to Heaven."

"Yes, those are the ones. And when we got married, we moved into her apartment but we're going to be needing a little bigger one soon."

Karen didn't seem to catch his hidden innuendo. "Tell me about the wedding. How was it? What were Lisa's colors?"

"The wedding was great. I'm not quite sure what her colors were. Do you mean what color of dresses the bridesmaids wore?"

"Don't worry about it. You're just like your father. Tell me everything else about the wedding."

Malachi remembered an amusing story. "We had pre-marriage counseling with Pastor Don before the wedding and, you are going to love this, Lisa asked him an interesting question about sex."

"How did he take it?"

"He fumbled here and there but finally pulled us back into our lesson. He did a great job at the wedding. He even mentioned how much Lisa reminded him of you."

"That's sweet. How did your father take that?"

Malachi reached back into his memory banks. "He got a little teary eyed but later claimed it must've been his allergies acting up."

"That's your father."

For a brief moment, Malachi felt transported back to his wedding and saw himself standing in front of the light blue carpeted sanctuary looking over at Lisa whose radiating beauty was accentuated by the satin white, shimmering wedding dress. While Pastor Don read off the powerful descriptions of love found in 1 Corinthians 13, Love is patient, love is kind, Malachi drifted to thinking about how his mother modeled all these noble traits.

Malachi was snapped back to the present with another question from Karen. "What about Lisa's family? What are they like?"

"They're great. Her mom and dad are neat people and we've become quite close. She has two younger brothers and I like to tease them a lot. Her youngest brother, Sam, plays basketball so I had to teach him some tricks."

"Honey, I am overjoyed for you. Remember, it takes a lot of work to have a healthy marriage. It doesn't just happen. Both people have to do their part and sometimes one has to do a little more but when you have a healthy marriage and include God in it, you will have peace and joy."

Malachi knew that his mom was sharing feminine insight that she would've provided had she been alive. "Mom, thank you. Yes, I'm very blessed to be married to Lisa. I married way above my station!"

"So did your father. Tell him that later."

Malachi was not sure if he would pass that on. "Uh, sure. Mom, tell me about Heaven. Does time pass slow? I mean do the five years in between our calls go quickly or do they seem to drag? Is it night then day? I have so many questions."

Karen appreciated Malachi's queries. "Honey, time was created on Earth for humanity. The Father created night and day and the seasons for people to be able to set schedules but here in Heaven, there are no time constraints. We are constantly surrounded with the radiant glory of the Lord. We are always joining the eternal celebration."

"Eternal celebration?"

Karen thought hard about an analogy he would understand. "O.K. honey, do you remember the Yellow Creek camp meeting that we went to when you were fourteen years old?"

"Oh yea, that's when I really got saved."

"That's right! And during the evening service, we were all together, you and your father and myself and we were worshipping. You turned to me and said, 'Mom, this is the best feeling I've ever felt. I wish we never had to leave here.' That honey is the best way I can describe Heaven to you."

"Wow."

"Wow indeed. Now quit trying to change the subject, I want to hear more about you and Lisa."

Malachi was still caught up in the fond memory of that incredible night at camp meeting. "Mom, she's wonderful. I'm sure Dad felt the same about you but being married to her is one of God's greatest gifts to me."

"Honey, I'm glad that you see it that way because God created marriage and it's one of the greatest gifts He gives to us."

"I guess, but if she doesn't start squeezing the toothpaste tube from the bottom, we might have problems."

"Honey, go get two tubes of toothpaste and don't make a big deal about it."

"Ha, ha, Mom, I'm sure that you and Dad had little pet peeves about each other."

"Malachi, you have no idea how long it took me to teach that man how to do laundry. And when I could get him to help, he would mix something red with the whites and everything came out pink."

"I can imagine Dad loved wearing pink clothes."

"He learned to do it the right way after that. Yes, honey, marriage can be tough but remember to keep God in the middle. He brought you two together and He'll keep you two together through the good and bad."

"Mom, is God allowing these phone calls so that you can teach me things about women?"

"Honey, the Father always knows what He's doing and it's amazing how it makes sense now. When I lived on earth there were many questions, but in Heaven, it all comes together."

"Wow, in some ways, I wish I was there with you."

"Honey, you will be here one day. Don't rush it. Enjoy every second that the Father grants you and when you do get here, you'll understand perfection. How is your Dad?"

"Dad's doing well, Mom. He was concerned about Lisa and I getting married and having student loans and he wanted us to wait a couple more years but he's fine now."

"Your father was just trying to make sure that you'd be all right. He didn't know that you had a job lined up at Anderson Middle School teaching Social Studies and that job is going well."

"Mom, at times, I forget that you're able to have glimpses of our lives here. So, you knew that I was working right after college?"

"Of course."

Malachi thought he would press Karen a little. "Well, then you know that Lisa is working as an accountant at a mortgage company. Will she get a raise soon?"

Karen's voice did not alter but assumed another tone. "Malachi, even if I knew what was going to happen, I wouldn't share it with you. That's not why we've been given this gift."

Malachi felt mildly reprimanded. "I'm sorry, I sort of was teasing but we would really like to know if she got her raise because she might not be working there too much longer."

"Oh, and why might Lisa not be working much longer? Is everything all right?"

"I see what you are doing, Mom. You're digging information out of me."

"I'm not quite sure what you mean, honey."

"Oh yes you do. You always knew how to drag things out of me. Remember in the first grade when Tim used to bully me and I was too scared to tell on him? But eventually you dragged it out of me. Then I learned you'd follow me to school and one day, you pulled him aside and scared him to death. I had no idea why he stopped bothering me."

"You should have seen the eyes bulge on that little boy. He was convinced that if he bullied you again, I was going to get him."

"Mom, I know, when Lisa and I were dating she reminded me that hell has no fury like a woman's scorn."

"She is a smart woman honey. Now, enough dodging, why might Lisa not be working much longer?"

"Mom, we think she's pregnant. We've taken a home test but we're going to the doctor tomorrow and find out for sure."

"I'm going to be a grandmother! Does Dad know? Does her parents know?"

"We've not told anyone else yet but are waiting until we hear something definite from the doctor."

"I am so proud of you. You will be a great father and Dad, oh I am worried about the dad, or would that be grandpa jokes? Please tell Lisa that I'm so excited."

"I love that you were the first one we told, Mom."

There are no tears in Heaven but Karen was close to bursting out with tears of joy. "Malachi, I think the gift of this phone call was for me this birthday."

"I don't know Mom, I really love this time together."

"I do too, but now it's time. Please take care of your beautiful wife and soon to be there beautiful child. And take care of your Dad too!"

Malachi became choked up and could not find words to respond and then he heard, "Never forget that I love you with all of my heart!" And the phone line went silent.

Minutes passed quickly as Malachi remained sitting back on their light gray recliner. As always, after a phone call with his mother, he replayed their conversation over and over in his mind as he didn't want to forget a single word or inflection of her voice. Entranced in deep recollection, Malachi didn't realize that tears started streaming down his cheeks.

After closing their first-floor apartment front door, Lisa turned and was slightly stunned as she saw that Malachi was crying. She rushed to him and wrapped her arms around him, "Are you all right?"

Malachi, yanked back into reality, answered her, "Yes, I'm fine."

"But you were crying. Did you and your mother not talk? Did the talk not go good?"

Malachi smiled, wiped off his tears, pulling his hand away looking at the wetness collected upon it as if he were surprised he had been crying. "Yes, we were able to talk and it was wonderful. I guess I was crying thinking about how if God is going to give such a great gift to me, then how much greater is Heaven? Then I started thinking about what a great gift I have in you Lisa. You mean so much to me! I love you."

Lisa let her yellow wind jacket slip to the floor and crawled up on Malachi's lap. "Now you are going to make me cry. I love you so much."

Lisa reached over with her left hand and guided Malachi's right hand unto her belly. "Tomorrow we are going to find out for sure about our little one."

"I told Mom about the baby and she is happy."

"I knew that she would be."

For a long time, Malachi and Lisa settled back together in the cushioned recliner and held each other.

# *Five*

MALACHI paused to look back as he was exiting the small hospital chapel lined with several colorful stained-glass windows portraying scenes of the life of Jesus. His last glimpse was of his father bowing his head as he sat on the small, red cushioned pew at the front of the tiny sanctuary. Right in front of Mike was a small, brown stained wooden table with the capital letters etched in, "Do This in Remembrance of Me" and several other symbols to encourage and assist those who ventured into the chapel.

Malachi grabbed the wooden door with both hands as he was closing it so that he wouldn't disturb his father spending time with God interceding for the family of his only son. As Malachi turned straight to get on the elevator to the third floor where the pediatric ward was located, he glanced to his right and saw the entrance to the small room where he and his father had been told of his mother's death.

Malachi involuntarily shook his head as he was reminiscing and calculating that it had almost been fifteen years since his mother went to Heaven. But Malachi did not have much time to dally as his wife, Lisa, was just about to give birth to their first child. Malachi and Lisa had intentionally decided they wouldn't find out the gender of their baby as they wanted to be surprised.

The elevator finally arrived on the third floor after what seemed to take an eternity on the second floor. Four visitors were caught up in a spirited discussion about the treatment their loved one was receiving and were caught off guard when they reached their destination. Malachi casually glanced toward the aluminum ceiling of the boxed elevator and wanted to interject his advice of "Get off the elevator. Argue about it in the hallway and let me continue. My wife is having a baby!" But he chose not to share his advice.

Finally, a loud ding sounded and the elevator sliding doors methodically opened allowing Malachi to escape its captivity. He took a right off of the elevator and stopped at a large, rounded desk where nurses appeared to be frantically scurrying. After approaching the circular, light orange desk, he was directed to a door that could only be passed through after a button was pushed to activate its opening and closing.

Malachi was looking up at the numbers on the doors as he was searching for number 8 where Lisa, and her mother, Rachel would be waiting. Rachel and her husband, Sam, arrived in Anderson from Wheeling a couple of days ago. Malachi and Sam were bombarded with a plethora of questions about if they agreed on this and that decision of the upcoming arrival of the new child.

"Malachi, Sam, what do you guys think? Should we paint the nursery a neutral color in the beginning or just pick one?" Rachel would question.

Both Malachi and Sam generally gawked at each other and abruptly shrugged their shoulders in a united manner and one would respond, "Whatever you two think, Dear."

Then as Rachel and a very pregnant Lisa rolled their eyes at the noncommitted response they received, Malachi and Sam winked at each other as they settled back watching the Reds baseball game on ESPN.

Every now and then, one of the girls would call out a random question from another room. "Should we put the crib in the right corner or the left corner?" Again, Sam taught his son-in-law well in that there were times when you just got out of the way and one of the men would answer, "Whatever you two feel is best."

Now the day had arrived and the little Byrge was going to make his or her presence known. Malachi saw room #8, not because he saw the small number directly in the middle of the top of the door, but because the sterile gowned future grandmother, Rachel, poked her head out and upon seeing Malachi, she barked, "Get in here! It won't take long now."

Malachi seemed to be taken back with those words of revelation and felt himself moving at warp speed to the metal cart beside the room door that was loaded with blue hospital gloves, flimsy yellow paper gowns, and tight-fitting face masks. When Malachi was fully adorned, he wondered if he appeared as a warrior about to enter battle but then also thought, he wasn't sure what he was getting himself into.

Entering Lisa's room, he quickly noticed the activity resembled a busy beehive. Two gowned nurses were in constant motion as a small electrical machine, with plastic black and red wires running back and forth was connected to Lisa. It was tapping out a loud rhythmic pattern of a small heartbeat and a dizzying array of numbers flashed back and forth across the tiny screen.

One of the nurses turned to Malachi. "All is well. We are calling the doctor because the baby will be here very soon."

Malachi looked over at Lisa and by the half smiling, half grimace spread across her flushed face, he wasn't sure if she wanted him to come closer or to cower quietly in a corner. His inexperienced paralysis was shattered when his excited mother-in-law snapped, "Malachi, go over there and hold your wife's hand." He dashed toward his wife making labored breathing sounds.

Malachi and Lisa had attended Lamaze classes and even practiced the hees and haas of the breathing technique at home but Malachi definitely was out of his element when they were in the labor room. He tried to comfort Lisa, "Hon, are you, all right?"

"Does it look like I'm all right?" Lisa bolted back and Malachi knew enough not to present a response but meekly replied, "I love you."

Lisa seem to soften a little as she tilted her head toward Malachi. "I love . . . " but then a major contraction jolted her body and she squeezed Malachi's hand tighter than it had ever been squeezed.

The tall doctor arrived and Malachi thought to himself, "He's acting much too calmly. Doesn't he know what is happening here?" But finally allowed himself to be assured that the doctor had probably delivered many babies and this was not his first time.

After four hours of labor, a healthy baby girl, Donna Jean, was ushered into the world. Malachi didn't know what emotions to have when he first saw her. He was overwhelmed, surprised, taken back at how little she was, and even found himself a little fearful. "What if I drop her? Lisa would probably be very mad at me."

When Malachi cradled his arms around his newborn daughter for the first time, he didn't know if he should laugh or cry so he did both. He gently rocked this precious piece of cargo in his arms and looked up at Lisa who had now melted back into the hospital bed completely drenched with sweat.

Their eyes made contact and Lisa mouthed, "I love you" and Malachi's eyes bounced back the same message as it echoed from his heart.

Later, Malachi found Mike still in the little chapel and announced, "You are a grandpa of a healthy little girl!" Mike jumped to his feet and ran to his son, still gowned in hospital apparel, and wrapped his arms around him. Sam had been waiting at their apartment as he did not feel comfortable waiting at the hospital. When he was called with the great news, he immediately jumped into his Ford truck and rushed to St. John's.

Malachi and Lisa had decided she would take a few years off work as they were building their family. Malachi's job was secure and his teaching ability was being recognized and rewarded. There were times when he wanted to get more involved with extracurricular school activities but always placed his family as his highest priority.

Soon, the nightly routine of waking up with Donna every few hours to feed her and make sure her soggy diapers were dry slowly dissolved into days where she was learning to wiggle back and forth like a top sized caterpillar.

But as every parent knows, newborn babies to quickly morph into months old babies and once they begin to walk, Mom and

Dad, need roller-skates to keep up with their constant motion. Things were well with the small family of Malachi, Lisa, and now Donna.

Before Donna entered the world and kept Malachi and Lisa busy, they had often talked of how many children they desired. After much discussion and negotiating, the number three was agreed upon. The toddler, Donna, was now a whirlwind of activity and had mastered the art of the word, "No." There were times when Malachi and Lisa looked at themselves and broke into laughter when Donna firmly crossed her tiny arms and said, "No!"

At the end of the school year, the eighth graders that Malachi was teaching had to pass a standardized State test which was designed to measure their overall comprehension and basic knowledge. Many of the teachers didn't care for it because they were concerned if a student did not pass, it may be a poor reflection upon themselves.

Two months before the test, the teachers systematically attempted to prepare the students without overloading them. It was during this pressing time that Malachi noticed that Lisa didn't seem to be feeling well and she often asked him to step in and intercede with their nonstop toddler.

One night, after Malachi finally wrangled Donna into her 'big girl' bed, read her a Bible story from the Egermeier's Family Bible, prayed with her, went back and forth three times to make sure she hadn't escaped from her little bed, he peered into her room and she had succumbed to slumber.

Malachi went back out to their living room and opened his black brief case that contained books of lessons, plucked one out, and was skimming through it wondering how he was going to teach all the material within it. Lisa poked her head around the hallway and her eyes danced as she playfully teased Malachi. "Do you want some news?"

Malachi rubbed his eyes as he thought about his wife acting mischievously. "Sure, wait a minute, what kind of news?"

Lisa fluttered her eyelashes at him. "Good news."

"I will always take good news. What's up?"

"We are going to have another baby!"

"A baby! What do you mean a baby? Wait. Who? Us?"

Lisa jumped onto his lap. "Yep."

Malachi found himself going into protective father mode. "Wow, but should you be jumping now?"

"I'm pregnant. I'm not a piece of China that will break if you drop it."

Malachi wrapped his arms around his wife. "Well you know that I would never drop you because I am going to hold you forever."

Many laughs and plans started that night and when they asked young Donna if she wanted a little brother or sister, she emphatically said, "No."

Phone calls to Mike and Sam and Rachel set off squeals of delight and instant plans started to emerge. Malachi and Lisa reminded them that they hadn't seen a doctor yet but were fairly convinced as they had found the pink cross on three pregnancy tests which announced that she was going to have another baby.

Rachel's motherly advice to Lisa was, "Please find out the gender this time. When baby Donna came, we had to repaint her room." Wanting confirmation and support, Rachel called out to Sam, "Isn't that right, honey?"

His response over the speaker phone caused both Malachi and Lisa to bust out laughing. "Whatever you think is right, dear."

When Mike heard the news, he became quiet and still causing Malachi to pause. "Are you all right Dad?"

Choked up and fighting tears, Mike replied, "I'm just thinking how proud I am of you and Lisa and how much your mother would've loved this."

Several months after the celebratory news was shared. Lisa was not feeling well physically. Often, with a concerned look on her face, she would curl up next to Malachi and say, "Honey, this one feels different than Donna. I hope everything is O.K."

"Honey, I'm sure that everything is fine."

But everything was not fine.

At 2:07 a.m. on a Sunday morning, Malachi was jolted out of a deep sleep when he heard Lisa's shrieks. Malachi shook his head to rid it of cobwebs and bolted toward the bathroom connected to their bedroom. As he opened the door, he saw his wife, Lisa huddled in a small pile near the bathtub and her green colored bathrobe was covered with bright red blood. Her face was streaked with countless tears and her arms wrapped around herself as she was slowly rocking.

Lisa had been spotting blood frequently during the pregnancy, but both she and Malachi were gently reassured from their obstetric gynecologist this was normal. Malachi rushed to his crumpled into a little ball wife and tenderly reached out to her. Lisa could only heartbreakingly mumble, "I think I lost the baby. I think I lost the baby."

Malachi shook his head as he was trying to come up with a plan. He had to figure something out to take care of his wife and unborn child. "Let's get to the hospital and we'll see what's going on."

Picking up a soundly sleeping Donna with one arm and trying to assist his wobbly wife, the pitiful looking entourage finally pulled into the rounded loop of the emergency room of St. John's Hospital.

With Lisa situated in her room, curled in a fetal position with an IV stuck in her arm, and nurses running back and forth, Malachi took the small hand of Donna into his and they stumbled back to the waiting room where Donna would soon be shifting into a small ball of energy.

Malachi called their next-door neighbor, Wes Easton to see if he and his wife April could come to the hospital and watch Donna so that Malachi could be with Lisa during this trying time. Wes quickly agreed and it wasn't long before he and April rushed into the waiting room, hugged Malachi tightly, and started distracting the now awake Donna.

It didn't take very long before a grim-faced doctor with a black rubber tubed stethoscope slung around his neck, announced to Malachi and Lisa she had suffered a miscarriage. The baby had passed. Malachi and Lisa did not know if it was shock or disbelief running through their souls as they blankly looked back at the doctor and thanked him.

A month later, the family, Mike, Rachel, Sam, Malachi, and Lisa, gathered together in support and with Pastor Don's spiritual guidance they were able to express their deep grief. Pastor Don suggested they name the unborn child to help identify and validate their sadness.

Lisa softly spoke, "His name is David Alan Byrge," and once again many tears spilled from the blood shot puffy eyes of the family.

The next few months seemed to be a blur as the upcoming state test was nearing and Malachi found himself jolted back to reality as he repeatedly thought about David. Lisa seemed to cope well as she busied herself with Donna and her new fascination with ponies. Often, Lisa and Donna would be found prancing up and down their hallway.

Malachi's 31st birthday was approaching and he found himself thinking how this was the fifth year and his mother, Karen, would be calling. There were times when Malachi found comfort knowing that he could tell his mom about Donna but also times of immense sadness when he didn't know what to say about David.

Malachi continually processed the many questions in his head with Lisa. "There is no sadness in Heaven so do I not say anything to Mom or what?"

The noncommittal look on Lisa's face betrayed her thoughts as she had no idea what to do either. She wanted to help Malachi but there were days when she found herself crying for no reason as the name David raced through her mind.

On Malachi's birthday, after a boring lunchtime meal of hotdogs and macaroni and cheese, Lisa and Donna started toward their bedroom, "We are going to try to take a nap and stay in our bedroom so we won't bother your phone call."

Malachi had never felt any other emotion about the phone calls from Heaven except for joy but for this one, he was hesitant and not sure what to tell his mother. Random inquiries ricocheted through his mind. "What if she senses I'm sad? What if I tell her and God stops the phone calls because there is no sadness in Heaven? What if I don't tell her and then later, she's hurt that I didn't say anything?" So many questions and Malachi could not come up with any answers.

He was snapped out of his pondering when his Samsung cell phone erupted into life with a very familiar ringtone. For a brief second, Malachi stared at it as the word, Heaven, flashed across the lit screen. "What if I don't answer it?" But he quickly dismissed that thought and slid the little green phone icon to the right.

"Happy Birthday my beautiful gift from God!" Malachi wasn't sure if his mother's voice seemed extra cheerful or if he was just being hypersensitive.

"Thank you, Mom, it's so good to hear your voice."

"We have a lot to talk about. How is your job? How is Lisa? Last time we talked, you told me you were going to have a baby!"

Malachi found himself feeling better talking with his mother but still wasn't sure what he should share and what he shouldn't divulge, "Work's great Mom. I love teaching. It was a little stressful the past couple of months because the kids had to pass that standardized test."

"So, how did they do?"

Malachi leaned back settling into the puffy cushioning of their pastel coach. "They did great. They all passed which took a lot of pressure off me."

"Well of course they did great. They had a great teacher."

"Now that's a comment only a mother could make."

"How is Lisa?"

"She's good, I mean, she's O.K. No, no, she's good."

Karen sensed Malachi was not being completely honest with her. "Honey, is there something that you are not telling me?"

Malachi felt torn as he wanted to keep talking to his mother but on the other hand, he felt trapped by what he should say and what he shouldn't say. All he came back with was, "No, Mom. Really everything is fine."

"Last time we talked you were about to have a baby. By the way, I just can't believe that you are 31 this year. You are a man, honey. I mean you really are a man."

"Thanks Mom, yes we had Donna Jean three years ago."

"Donna Jean!" Karen exclaimed, "That's the name of your great-grandmother."

"I know Mom, that's who we named her after, your grandmother."

"And Grandma Donna is doing wonderful here in Heaven."

"Grandma Donna? You mean you've seen her?"

"Oh yes honey. Part of the beauty of Heaven is reuniting with loved ones and spending time with them as we worship the Father. So, tell me everything about little Donna Jean."

"Oh Mom, she's beautiful and smart but stubborn."

"So she's like her father and grandfather?"

Malachi laughed, and it felt good to laugh. "Hey, we resemble that remark."

"Tell me everything about her. What does she like? What's her personality like? Does she look like Lisa?"

"Mom, she is always moving. She wears us out. She loves ponies and when we say her prayers at night, she always asks for one."

"I know, her prayers are special."

"What do you mean Mom? Can you hear our prayers?"

"Like we have talked about before, the Father allows us to have glimpses of your life and one of my favorite times is when I see you kneeling beside her little bed praying. By the way, honey, is she big enough to have a bed like that or should she still be in a crib?"

Malachi didn't want to correct his mother but replied, "She's all right Mom."

"Remember, she's my first grandchild, I can be a little overbearing if I want."

"That's true, how many grandmothers in Heaven are chewing out their sons about their grandchildren?"

"What does she like to do?"

"Mom, she runs and runs and runs and then plays and plays and plays and when we think that she's winding down, she asks us a million questions."

"Honey, enjoy her at this age because when she gets a little older, it gets harder."

"Are you saying that as I got older, I was hard to deal with?"

"Honey, I don't think you want me to remind you about the time you were eight and you ran across that busy street to swing on the outside playset in front of Lowes. Oh, and when you were eleven, you were so mad at your father and I that you were going to run away but as you were storming out of the house, you turned and said, 'Find me in an hour because I'll be hungry.'"

Malachi was now laughing out loud, which felt good because he had not been very happy lately. "O.K. Mom, enough war stories. Besides, I'm not really sure if I said that when I was eleven."

"Oh honey, you said it. Because when you closed the door your father and I fell over laughing."

"Mom, I know I put you and Dad through a lot. I'm learning how hard it is to be a parent with Donna."

"Honey, you will be learning how to be a parent for the rest of your life. The most important thing to do is to raise them to know God."

"Mom, I have a wonderful relationship with God because I saw it in your life and I see it in Dad's."

"That's such a sweet thing to say. How is Dad?"

"He's good. He just had a really hard time when . . . ," and Malachi stopped.

"He had a hard when what?"

"Well Mom, even though we've talked every five years since I've been sixteen there are still a lot of things that I don't understand about our phone calls."

"What do you mean, honey? What things don't you understand?"

Malachi brushed his right hand through his hair as he felt he blew it. "Well, you know, we can't talk about anything sad."

"I don't remember ever saying that we can't talk about anything sad."

"I thought you said that you're not sad in Heaven."

"Yes, that's true but I also told you that if I hear anything sad in our conversations the Father is going to show me how it will work out so I ultimately won't be sad."

Malachi surrendered. "Mom, I do have some sad news."

"Honey, what's wrong?"

Malachi fondly remembered many times when his mother was on earth and she asked him that very question. "Mom, Lisa and I lost a baby."

Karen's response shocked Malachi. "I was hoping you were going to mention David. I didn't want to bring him up before you did."

"David? How did you know his name?"

"Oh, and he's not lost. He and I run around together. He is so handsome. He looks so much like you. He is the most beautiful grandson a woman could ever have."

"What are you talking about Mom? David died before he was born."

Karen corrected him. "No, son, he did not die. He came to Heaven to be with his grandma. He sits on my lap and we giggle and giggle."

Malachi felt wetness stream from his eyes and realized that he was crying. "Mom, David is in Heaven with you?"

"Oh yes, the night at the hospital when you were walking Donna to the waiting room, he came to Heaven. Instantly he was in the arms of Jesus and when Jesus put him down, he ran into my arms saying, 'Nana.'"

Malachi felt his head swirling. "He knew you? But he was only a little embryo. He hadn't been born yet."

"Yes but when he arrived in Heaven, he received his new body and he and I run around. Remember Grandma Donna, she really likes him."

"Mom it means so much to me that he's with you. I've really been hurting."

"I know, so many times I wished we could talk more so that I could've told you that he's doing fantastic."

Malachi felt a pressure relieved much like the thick concrete walls of a hydraulic dam letting loose thousands of gallons of water and he let out a loud, "Praise God."

"Honey, God works all things out for the good of those who love Him and when you and Lisa get here, you'll understand."

At that point, Malachi was startled because he suddenly looked up and Lisa was standing in the living room looking forlorn with her arms crossed. "Mom, Lisa is in the living room right now. Can I tell her about David?"

Karen stopped for a second and Malachi heard her asking a question not directed toward him and then she quickly answered him, "Malachi, if she is willing to talk to me, put her on the phone."

Malachi objected. "But wait a minute, I thought that only I could hear you?"

"Again the Father is so good to His children that He's allowing me just this once to talk to Lisa."

Malachi looked over at Lisa and extended the phone towards her in shock. "Would you like to talk to my mother?"

Lisa's body posture immediately shot to a straight position and she tilted her head back. "What do you mean, talk to your mother?"

Malachi shook the phone toward her as he shrugged his shoulders. "She wants to talk to you."

Lisa cautiously took the phone from Malachi without lifting her eyes from him in a suspicious manner. She hesitated and looked at the caller id on the screen and it read, Heaven, "Hello?" It was almost a question instead of a greeting.

"Hi, you must be the one who stole my little boy's heart."

"Um, I guess I did, who am I talking to?"

"It's Karen, Malachi's mother."

"But I thought only Malachi could hear you?"

"Yes, that's true, but the Father allowed another special gift for me to talk to you."

Lisa found herself with as many questions as there were stars in the sky. "But why me?"

"Honey, it's because you are hurting. I'm so sorry that David wasn't with you very long."

Now Lisa was really reeling. "How do you know about David?"

"He's here with me right now. After our phone call, we'll go join the legions of angels in worship."

Lisa almost felt lightheaded. "I'm sorry, our son David? The baby we lost, is with you right now in Heaven?"

"Yes," Karen answered and went on, "But you didn't lose him, he came to Heaven with his grandmother, me."

Lisa found tears slipping down her face. "So, he's O.K.?"

"He's more than O.K. and he reminds me so much of his father, your husband. He moves like him and there are times when I catch myself thinking, he even sounds like him."

Lisa sank down to a seated position next to the wall. "Karen, or Mom, or what do I call you? You don't know how much this phone call has helped."

"You can call me Mom but don't ever think I'm an overbearing mother-in-law checking on you from Heaven."

Lisa laughed as she was trying to understand what was taking place. "Are there a lot of overbearing mothers-in-law in Heaven?"

"Oh, I see why Malachi loves you. You have a sense of humor like him. Please give the phone back to Malachi as our time is up and we'll probably not be able talk again until you get to Heaven but know that David is good and he's keeping his Nana company."

Tears were cascading from Lisa's eyes as she handed the phone back to Malachi. Malachi kept looking at his wife and was trying to figure out if the tears were happy or sad. "Hi Mom, so you met Lisa."

"Honey, she is beautiful. I'm so happy for both of you and the Father wanted her to know that David was in good hands. Well, our time is up."

"Mom, I love you!"

Then the words, "Never forget that I love you with all of my heart," rang through the phone and it was silent.

Lisa's eyes were not blinking as she asked Malachi, "Did I just talk to your mother in Heaven?"

"Yep. It's great, isn't it?"

Lisa moved over and sat on Malachi's lap. "It's more than great. I really needed that. Our son, David is running around with his grandmother in Heaven."

"There is no telling what trouble those two could be causing."

Cuddling together, their conversation was interrupted by a little prancing pony whose sun kissed hair bounced as she galloped toward them and Donna, with childlike wonder, asked, "Why Mommy sad?"

Lisa wiped the watery streaks from her face and pulled Donna into her and Malachi and said, "Mommy's not sad. I'm happier than I've been in a while and do you know why?"

Donna snuggled in closely, grabbing her father's much larger hand to fiddle with it. "Why, Mommy?"

"Because God loves us so much and He loves you!" Lisa slowly stroked the blonde hair of her daughter.

Donna fiddled out of their tender clutches and said, "I love Him too and now Daddy, come to my room and tell me a story about Him."

Malachi picked up his precious daughter and looked lovingly at his wife, "Tonight honey, we are going to talk about Heaven." And he gently placed her over his shoulder in a playful manner as she kicked her feet in delight.

# *Six*

A FEW days before Malachi's 36th birthday, he found himself not sleeping well. In between tossing one way and turning the other, he felt like a spinning top someone had twisted and shot into a speeding twirling motion. One night, he woke up completely drenched in sweat as perspiration plastered his soaked hair to the side of his face and moisture ran down the back of his cotton t-shirt. It took a while before he could slow down his racing pulse and calm the pounding of his heart.

He also noticed that he was having several bad dreams. Normally his dreams were pleasant and he rarely remembered them but these were etched deeply into the memory banks of his mind.

In one dream, Malachi had dropped his phone and it fell into a deep, dark hole and he jumped into the unknown chasm to retrieve it. Malachi recalled that the phone was just out of reach and he kept trying to grab it again and again. The very top of his extended fingertips were so close to the plummeting phone but not close enough. The bottomless void had no end so Malachi thought he was going to be reaching for his phone forever.

The second dream was somehow, someone had stolen Malachi's phone and was impersonating him. In the dream, Malachi couldn't see the caller as he or she was lurking in an impenetrable shadow. Malachi could make out an outline of a menacing figure but never see anything or anyone clearly. Whoever, or whatever, had taken his phone was calling Malachi's friends and family and spewing lies about him and his family.

Malachi seemed paralyzed and helpless as the action unfolded. He couldn't move his hands to reach the brazen thief or move his feet to walk toward him or her. His vocal chords were seized so he wasn't even able to cry out for him or her to stop. Helplessness flooded over Malachi and all he could do was stand by as an unwilling victim.

The morning of his 36th birthday, Malachi couldn't remember any of his dreams the previous evening but felt haunted by them. A residue of fear slowly crept through his heart. Thoughts darted through his mind, "What's going on here? What's the matter with me?" Weakly, Malachi forced his feet to the ground, stretched his aching neck as far back as possible, pulled the blanket away, and made himself rise to a standing position.

Thankfully, it was a Saturday so he didn't have to go to school but found himself occasionally sinking into a mental fog. "What was I just doing?"

Lisa noticed that Malachi was not himself and tried to cheer him up. "Happy Birthday honey! We are going to have a little party this afternoon for you."

"Don't you remember that this is the day when my mom is going to call me?"

Lisa's body language showed that she was taken back a little. "Of course, honey, we won't have your party until 4:00 or 5:00, whatever works best for you." Pausing, Lisa added, "Are you all right?"

Malachi caught himself in his doldrums and wasn't happy he barked at Lisa. "I'm sorry babe. I haven't been sleeping well lately."

"I know. I'm on the other side of the bed."

"Come here. I'm sorry. I'll figure out what's going on."

Lisa snuggled into his embrace. "O.K., in an hour, we'll be out of your hair and come back after 3:00 and then we'll figure out the rest about your party."

"I love you. You are the one of the greatest gifts God has ever given me."

A flirty smirk crossed Lisa's face. "Don't you ever forget that." And she playfully gave him a quick kiss on the lips and pushed away from him.

1:17 p.m. was rapidly approaching and Malachi couldn't remember where he put his phone. Normally, he placed it on the edge of their marble counter in the kitchen right next to their stainless-steel refrigerator. He kept it there so that he would always know where it was if he needed it. But today, it wasn't there.

A small panic gripped Malachi. "What if I can't find my phone? I'll miss Mom's call." An urgency pulsed through Malachi and he found himself frantically going room to room. When he was nearing his bedroom, he suddenly recalled that he left it on his wood-stained nightstand so that it would be next to him. With all of the dreams having something to do with his phone, he didn't want it to be too far away from him.

Sitting on the edge of his bed, Malachi cupped the smartphone in his hand and noticed it was 1:15 p.m., two minutes and his mother would be calling. The two minutes passed slowly and as each second marched by, Malachi developed another doubt if he would hear from his mother today.

Malachi sighed a breath of relief when the phone came to life because his apprehensions of doom hadn't transpired. He slid the green icon to the right, "Hello."

"Happy Birthday, my beautiful gift from God!"

Malachi found himself fighting back tears. "Mom, it's so good to hear your voice!"

"Honey, it's been a little rough on you lately, hasn't it?"

"Mom, I don't know what's going on. I can't sleep. I'm having weird, terrible dreams."

Karen listened intently and then launched into teaching. "Honey, you know that there's an enemy, right?"

"An enemy? Do you mean the devil?"

"That's exactly who I mean. He wants to rob you of joy and peace and he's constantly working. Lately, he's had his hooks in you."

Malachi leaned back and pulled his feet up on the bed and stretched out. "So, that's why I've been having these weird dreams and not sleeping."

"Yes, so please know that they'll stop because he's been trying to convince you that I wouldn't call you this birthday."

An aha moment dawned on Malachi. "Of course. That's why every bad or crazy dream involved my phone."

"Now you are seeing it. The enemy's job is to discourage you and get you to look away from the goodness of the Father. The gift of these phone calls is an incredible gift from Him to us and so naturally, the enemy wants to try to shut them down."

Malachi slowly rose to a seated position. "But the devil . . . he can't stop these, can he?"

"Oh no, no, honey. The devil has been defeated but he sure makes a lot of noise. The Father always keeps His promises to us."

"Mom, I feel better already. I do feel I've been put through the ringer." Malachi kicked his feet over the bed planting them on the floor.

"Honey, tell me everything that's happened the last five years. Don't leave anything out."

"Wow, oh Mom, so much has happened. Work is great. I love teaching. Lisa is great and Donna just turned six years old and she has life all figured out and Kimberly is running around now."

"Kimberly? I haven't heard of a Kimberly before."

"Oh, I'm sure. I know that you've been watching and saw when we had our second daughter."

"Of course we did. David and I were jumping around when Kimberly came into the world. David wasn't thrilled at first at having two sisters but he figures he'll be able to show them around Heaven someday."

"David? How is my son?"

"Just like you and Lisa. He is the best of both of you put together. So, tell me all about Kimberly."

Malachi, not sure where to start, took a deep breathe. "Well, she's very different than her big sister Donna. Donna is pretty confident and likes to share that confidence with others."

"So, she's bossy."

"Well, I'm not sure if the word bossy fits. Well, yes it does."

"But Kimberly, she's more calm and relaxed. She doesn't get excited too easily even though she's only four years old. When Donna was younger, her main word was no but Kimberly just smiles a lot."

"How do the girls get along?"

"Like sisters. For the most part, Donna tries to tell Kimberly what to do and Kimberly just smiles at her and then they run off and play together."

"I love being in Heaven but I do wish that I would've been able to hold the girls."

"Mom, can you have regrets in Heaven?"

"No, no, honey. Heaven is saturated with so much love that we're complete. I know that there will be a day when I'll be able to hold my family again so I don't have any regrets."

"Mom, do you know when we'll be coming to Heaven?"

Karen reminded Malachi of things she had explained earlier in their initial phone calls. "Now you remember there are things that you won't understand and things I can't share with you."

"O.K., O.K., I won't push"

"How is your shoulder doing?"

"Oh, it's doing really well. Right after the therapy it started feeling better."

"Therapy?"

"I see what you're doing. You're prying into what happened because I hadn't told you I had to have shoulder surgery and then therapy. I thought you would've known."

"Yes, I knew but remember, I want to hear about it from you. Your surgeon was very nice and the operation went well."

"Were you able to see the operation?"

"Of course. Since my son was having surgery I wanted to make sure I watched."

Malachi thought back how his father and Lisa were huddled on the dark green suede chairs in the hospital waiting room with the television loudly blaring one of the cable news stations and his mother was in Heaven watching the surgery. "I guess you were. I hadn't thought about it."

"Now O.K., Malachi Edward, why did you have to have the surgery?"

Malachi hemmed and hawed. "You know Mom."

"Yes, I do know but I want to hear it from you."

"I was playing third base on the church softball team and was probably throwing the ball too hard."

"You might have been throwing the ball too hard?"

Malachi felt he was twelve years old again and had left the milk out of the refrigerator and was receiving a lecture about spoiled milk. "I know Mom."

"Honey, you are not 20 years old anymore. You need to start taking it easy."

"I know Mom. Trust me, I know."

"So the girls are good? How is Lisa?"

Malachi stood and started walking back to the living room. "Mom, she's good. She is so wonderful. I snapped at her earlier and she called me on it. She just makes me better."

Karen launched into a theological discourse. "That's why the Father created her for you. She's your helpmate. She encourages you and builds you up. That's why marriage was created. The Father saw you men and said, 'They need some help' and that's why He created Eve."

Malachi wasn't going to just sit by and let men be bashed. "Yes, we need help but if Eve wasn't with us, we would still be in the garden of Eden in a perfect place, racing the cheetahs and high fiving the monkeys."

"Very funny, don't blame Eve. Adam was standing right there with her."

"I know Mom. I remember the story."

"Just don't ever forget how precious Lisa is."

"I won't Mom."

"How is your father? Has he retired yet?"

Malachi had hoped he might not come up in their conversation. "Dad, yea Dad, he's good. About retirement, he has another couple of years to work and will probably be done at 62. You know that he is 60 now?"

"I know, I just can't believe it. 60 years old. When we were younger, 60 seemed so old. But honey, know that 60 is really not that old."

"Oh Mom, trust me, I know. Now that I'm getting older, 60 seems very young."

"You are not getting older. You will always be my little man."

Malachi cringed. "Mom, you know that I hated when you called me that. Dad always told me that when you're a man you have to work all day and pay taxes and not have any fun and then you would tell me I was a man."

"You used to turn red and clamp your fist together and say, 'I'm not a man, I'm a boy. I want to have fun.'"

Malachi cackled at that fond memory.

"So Dad will be retiring. Anything else going on with him?"

Malachi truly found himself at a loss for words. In his mind, he thought, "She has to know. Obviously, she knows."

"Hmm? What else is going on with your father?"

"Mom, you know."

"I know what honey?"

Malachi felt like a pent-up pressure valve about to explode. "You know Mom."

"You keep saying that. Why don't you just say it?"

Malachi acknowledged defeat. "Mom, you were always a pain when you kept pushing me to tell you things. You know that Dad has remarried."

"Honey, I'm sorry, I was just having fun with you. Yes, I know your father has remarried and she's a very nice person."

"If you knew then why did you keep giving me a hard time?"

"Oh honey, I told you I was just having fun, besides why was it so hard for you to tell me about Dad getting remarried?"

Malachi plopped onto their living room recliner and pulled the wooden lever to extend the footrest. "Mom, I didn't know how you would take it."

"Honey, I want what is best for you and your father. I'm a little surprised that he didn't get remarried much earlier."

"He really had a hard time dealing with you going to Heaven. And for a long time, he felt guilty about thinking of another woman."

"Malachi, I came to Heaven at a young age and your father was young. It would've been perfectly fine if he would've had another relationship sooner."

"So, you understand?"

"Of course, I understand. Tina is a wonderful woman and she loves the Lord and will help your father be the man that God wants him to be."

Now it was Malachi's turn to ask questions. "So you know about Tina and you know that she's a Godly woman, isn't it a little hard for you?"

"Malachi, you want what is best for Lisa, don't you?"

Malachi quickly responded, "Yes."

"I want what is best for your dad too."

"O.K. Mom, but what about when Dad and Tina get to Heaven? Who is he going to be married to?"

"Get into your Bible, honey."

Several years ago, this question came up in Sunday School and Malachi researched it but found different theologians had a different understanding and teaching on the subject. "Mom I have looked this up and I'm pretty confused about it."

"Honey, in Heaven, there is no confusion. Every one of your answers will be cleared up and you'll completely understand."

"But I'm really curious, are you both going to be married to Dad?"

"Honey, I'm not sure if any man could really handle two wives."

"Mom, I'm serious, I have been wrestling with this since Dad got remarried," Malachi blurted out.

"Honey, it's not something you have to be concerned about. O.K., I'll break it down for you like this. The Church is made up of Christians, right? The Church is not really the brick-and-mortar buildings and the padded chairs and long pews and the stained-glass windows. The Church is the body of Christ, the believers."

"O.K., I understand that but what does that mean?"

"What in the Bible is the Church or Christians called?"

"We are the bride of Christ. He is our bridegroom."

"Yes, exactly. When we get to Heaven, we still recognize each other and love each other but we are the Bride of Christ."

Malachi slowly repeated what he thought he heard. "So we are married to Jesus?"

"Yes, exactly. We're able to see each other and know each other and remember the good times and we love each other but we're overwhelmed by the glory of the Father and Son and Holy Spirit . . . "

Malachi interrupted. "Overwhelmed? I'm not sure what you mean we're overwhelmed by the glory of the Trinity?"

"Honey, I'm almost giving you too much. You're very smart. You've always been but when we're on earth we have a very limited comprehension about God."

"Yes, I know, now we know in part but then we shall fully know. I know the Bible verse."

"That's true, honey, Heaven is so incredible. Think about the most peaceful time you've ever had in your life. Think about the most joyful time you've ever had. Think about the most incredible moment in your life, put them all together and that's what Heaven is like."

"One of the most joyful times was watching the girls being born. Mom, when they came into the world, I don't think I could've been happier."

"Yes, remember that joy and that's what Heaven is like all the time."

Malachi was seriously contemplating what his mother had said. "And Mom, probably one of the most peaceful times I've ever had was your first phone call to me after you went to Heaven."

"It's so hard to think that was twenty years ago today but that shows you how the Father can give us a peace even when we are hurting."

"Mom, there is so much more that I want to learn about Heaven."

"I know but remember the little that I've shared with you because when you arrive you'll be amazed for eternity."

Malachi sensed their phone call would soon be ending. "But Mom, I have so many more questions. What about . . . "

Karen stopped him midsentence. "You always were so inquisitive. Honey, just know that Heaven is a perfect place and we're waiting for you and Lisa and the girls and your father and yes, your new mother."

"She will never replace you Mom."

"No, honey, but love and respect her and know there will be a day when we'll all worship together."

Malachi pushed the lever strapped on the side of the recliner down. "Mom, all I can say is wow."

"Yes, and one day we'll all be saying wow together."

Malachi knew their time was short. "Mom, I love you."

And once again, Malachi heard the familiar closing refrain, "Never forget that I love you with all of my heart", and the phone went silent.

Malachi had pushed himself to a seated position on the edge of the straightened-up recliner and stared blankly at the wall ahead. He had so many questions about Heaven and each time his mother answered one, he had more. In Malachi's heart, he accepted how wonderful and magnificent Heaven was but in his mind he wanted to know more and more.

Malachi's time of reflection was quickly interrupted as he heard Lisa unlock their front door and push it open. When she did, instantly two little girls bolted toward their father and jumped up toward him. With both arms, Malachi corralled his girls and nestled them closely.

Donna lowered her head and peered directly at her father. "Daddy, today is your birthday and we have presents for you. I wanted to get you a new wallet but Mommy made me buy you a belt. Do you need a belt? I hope so. Later, we're going to have a party and if you need help blowing out your candles, I will do it."

Malachi was attempting to match the serious look on his daughter's face but couldn't and a wide grin burst upon his face. "Sweetie, you're not supposed to tell people what presents you get them."

Donna wasn't about to slow down. "Daddy, I didn't tell you. I just told you that Mommy didn't let me get the wallet."

Malachi pulled her closer and looked at Kimberly, "What do you think honey? Are you ready for a party?"

Kimberly's face beamed with a beautiful smile and Donna answered for her, "She says she's ready." Then Malachi gathered Kimberly closer and tickled her.

Lisa broke up the festivity. "O.K., girls, let's go into my bedroom and we'll do, you know what, and start getting ready for the party."

As Donna was squirming out of her father's grip, she whispered, "You know that means we have to wrap your presents." And Kimberly excitedly shook her head nodding it up and down in agreement.

After much sticky scotch tape and multi-colored ribbon and blue wrapping paper was thrown together concealing Malachi's presents, the girls rejoined him in the living room as he watched ESPN.

As Lisa came out, she told Malachi, "Hon, I talked to your dad and Tina and they'll be here around 5:00. Do you still want spaghetti for your birthday dinner?"

Malachi's eyes opened largely. "Spaghetti, mmm, mmm." As he balanced the two girls climbing back on him again.

Donna leaned toward her father and cupped her little hand next to her mouth. "Daddy, who is Tina?"

Malachi cast a glance over at Lisa who was standing next to the pantry in the kitchen. "Yes Mommy, who is Tina?"

Grabbing a box of pasta noodles as she pulled her head out of the wooden cabinet. "Tina is Grandma Byrge."

Kimberly piped up like a small bird chirping, "Grandma Byrge?"

Donna lifted her eyes at her mother, "I thought she was in Heaven."

Malachi knowing that Lisa wanted him to rescue her interceded, "You are right, Grandpa's first wife is in Heaven and we can call her Nana and we call his second wife, Grandma."

Donna seemed perplexed. "How many wives does a man get?"

With this question, Lisa stopped pouring the noodles into the large metal pan on their stove and smirked. "Yes, Daddy, how many wives does a man get?"

Malachi closed his eyes tightly causing both girls to giggle. "Oh, I don't know. I just want one. I just want Mommy."

As Lisa turned back to the stove whose enamel surface was heating up, she in a low voice quipped, "Good answer, mister."

"Did you say something dear?"

"Nothing you don't already know sweetie." And both girls looked at each other and rolled their eyes.

After watching the sports replays of the best double plays from earlier games, Malachi asked Lisa if she needed any help and she replied, "No, this is your birthday and in about an hour our guests will be here."

Right at 5:00 p.m., Mike and Tina knocked briskly on the front door and Malachi lifted the girls in his arms and carried them like they were sacks of potatoes. Lisa saw this and ran to the door and opened it and Mike and Tina were greeted by squealing girls in tow.

Mike, his once brown hair now completely white, and moving a little slower, burst out, "How are my favorite two granddaughters?"

Malachi bent over and gently placed the girls to a standing position and stood back up and embraced his father while Donna accurately pointed out, "Grandpa, we are your only granddaughters."

Mike wiggled out of Malachi's embrace and with a gleam in his eye. "That means that you are my favorite, favorite granddaughters," and Kimberly smiled.

Lisa leaned in and embraced Tina and then Mike and offered to take their coats. After handing over a light brown suit jacket and a pink windbreaker, Lisa walked to their room to place their coats on their bed.

Mike sized up his son. "36 years old! That's old. My, my, my and you are already falling apart," motioning toward his shoulder.

Malachi rotated the shoulder that had surgery. "Don't I know it. Tina, how are you?"

She smiled and leaned in and hugged Malachi. "I'm well. Happy Birthday."

Lisa then returned and motioned for everyone to come in and have a seat as everything was ready. Donna grabbed her father's hand and said, "This is your party." Kimberly looked up at her father and took hold of his other hand.

As he was escorted by two little princesses, he thought about the joy of Heaven and wondered if he would remember this particular joyful memory. After the festive occasion of eating the wonderful meal that Lisa prepared and blowing out candles on the cake and unwrapping presents, Lisa told the girls, "Give everyone a hug because it's bath time since we have church tomorrow."

The girls squeezed and loved on all those sitting around the table and their laughter was contagious. As Lisa was heading down the hallway, she suggested, "Malachi, why don't you and Mike and Tina sit in the living room?" The men looked at each other in agreement.

Tina stood up and was collecting the dishes and told Malachi and Mike, "You two go in there. I will start cleaning up."

Mike and Malachi settled into respective recliners and Mike turned to his son, "Malachi, I am very proud of you. I don't think that I could've had a better son."

In order for his father not to see his eyes moisten, Malachi turned to see the baseball action the television screen. "Thanks Dad and I couldn't have had a better father."

Lisa, with soap suds clinging to the side of her damp blouse said, "The girls will be in to say goodnight soon. Tina, you shouldn't have started cleaning up."

"It was my pleasure."

Two little pajama clad girls paraded into the living room where dad and grandpa were sitting and shook their still mildly wet heads and giggled. Then they rushed back into their rooms.

With the girls in their rooms and Lisa and Tina still in the kitchen, Mike quietly asked Malachi, "Did your mother call you today?"

"Yes, she did."

"You know, I still don't understand those phone calls."

"I really don't either, Dad."

Mike seemed like he wanted to say something but was holding back so Malachi pressed him. "Anything you want to ask me Dad?"

"Did she ask about me?"

At first Malachi thought he would tease his father and answer, "Of course not." But then he decided not to be mean. Instead he answered, "Yes, Dad, she always asks about you but then she already knows what's going on with us."

Mike sat up straighter. "What did she ask?"

Malachi knew what his father wanted to know. "Dad, she knows about Tina and she is very happy for you. She loves you and wants what's best for you."

A solitaire tear streamed down from Mike's eye. "You know I will always love your mother."

Malachi sincerely looked over at his father. "I know Dad."

For a brief moment, Mike thought about Karen but then blurted out to Malachi, "You know I don't know about this marriage in Heaven thing though."

Malachi almost tipped over in the recliner. "Dad, don't get me started."

# Seven

"WHAT now?" Malachi forcefully slapped the wooden kitchen table with his open palm creating a loud 'smack'. Malachi's frustration had peaked and the girls were about to bear the brunt of an internal explosion.

As Malachi rose and pushed himself away from the table, he immediately launched into a rambling diatribe. "How many times have I told you girls to stop fighting?" It was much more than a rhetorical question but an emotional regurgitation of exasperation.

As Malachi briskly marched down the hallway toward the young offenders, he surprised himself at his anger and how quick he was to snap. When he arrived at Donna's bedroom, two pairs of young eyes were wide open not knowing what to expect from their raging father.

Donna and Kimberly were normal young girls, Donna now a preteen, eleven years old, trying to grow up too fast and Kimberly, being nine, knew exactly how to push the right button of her sister to illicit a reaction. But both girls found themselves swimming in stunned astonishment at how their normally calm father now seemed like a multi-headed fiery dragon spewing lava like streaks of flames.

When Malachi saw their shocked expressions, a tinge of remorse intermingled with sensibility started to overtake him. "Girls, you know Dad has a lot going on and I really need you two not to fight and argue."

Donna rapidly pleaded her defense as if she were testifying in a court of law. "Dad, I wasn't doing anything and Kimberly came into my room and grabbed my phone."

As Donna was defending her behavior, Kimberly stuck her tongue out at her and shot back, "Dad, she said I could look at it for a little bit."

"That's before you started being a brat!" And Donna pronounced the word brat as if it were a curse word only the seediest of characters used.

Kimberly's tongue once more shot out of her tiny mouth as if it were a sharpened dagger plunging directly into her sister.

With Donna glaring at Kimberly, Malachi tried to reason with the two little combatants, "Girls, Mom and Dad have a lot on our plates. You know it's been hard since Dad has gone back to school and Mom is working part time. We wish it were easier but for a little longer, we need your help."

When Malachi turned forty years old, he learned of an educational program offered to tenured teachers to pursue a master's degree. It was an accelerated set of classes but after two years, he would not only receive an advanced degree but also be rewarded a needed pay raise. After much discussion, Malachi and Lisa together decided he should do it.

Three months before this unexpected opportunity arose, Lisa went back to work as a bookkeeper for a local construction company. She only worked three days a week, Tuesday, Wednesday, and Thursday, from nine to five and the extra money she earned helped provide for the household expenditures.

Both Malachi and Lisa were aware and believed they'd be able to face the new changes of her working and him studying and writing assigned papers and be all right. For the most part, things were proceeding nicely. Though occasionally, their lives felt as if they hit a concrete speedbump and quickly careened off the road.

Today was one of those days. Malachi had a test approaching and was attempting to study. Lisa was at work, and the girls were, well, they were being girls.

Malachi knelt down and gathered the girls in his arms pulling them into a tight huddle. "O.K. girls, we are just going to stay like this until you two get along."

Donna, trying to fight back a case of the giggles, stated, "We are probably going to be here forever then."

All wrapped together, a smile erupted on Kimberly's face. "Donna, I'm sorry."

Donna, still wanting to act cool. "It's O.K. Just ask next time if you want to look at my phone."

Malachi snuggled in closer with each girl. "Now you see, how hard was that? Please you two, get along. I have a big test this week and when it's over we'll go to the park on Saturday. Can you do that for me?"

Both girls nodded their heads in affirmation and Malachi kissed each on the forehead and stood up. "Dad has a lot to go over today and Mom will be home in about an hour."

As he exited Donna's room, Malachi felt he should be awarded the father of year award as he was taking advanced classes, teaching school, and holding down the fort when Lisa was away. He soon settled back onto the white wooden chair at the table and opened the Medieval history book trying to find his place again.

For a brief time, Malachi was able to arduously study how the medieval historical time period ushered in the Renaissance and was putting it all together. But once again his intense concentration was broken by a shrill shriek and the pattering sound of retreating footsteps.

"Dad, Kimberly just ran into my room and threw a doll at me," tattled Donna.

"Dad, she called me a brat again," Kimberly vociferously countered.

"Dad, she is being a brat again."

Malachi thought that the peaceful tranquility would last, at least, until Lisa came home from work but he was wrong. He shouted from the table, "Girls, I thought we were going to get along?"

Both girls simultaneously chattered, "But Dad . . . "

Malachi interrupted them. "No buts, we agreed that we would get along."

From the hallway, Malachi heard the sarcastic underlaying rebellion of Donna. "I don't remember agreeing to get along with that brat."

As Malachi again rose from the table and headed toward the hallway, he snapped. "Young lady, watch your tone and your attitude and quit calling your sister a brat."

Kimberly was delighted that the rains of rebuke were streaming down upon her sister. "Yea, Dad, tell her."

Malachi, now standing in front of both young girls in the hallway, barked, "You stop too. You know that you're winding up your sister to get her mad."

With this reprimand, Donna wiggled her scrunched up face mocking her sister and like a breaker in a fuse box noisily short circuiting, Kimberly stepped up and raised her hand to swat her sister. Malachi quickly stepped between them separating the tiny warriors.

Malachi screamed, "Girls, we do not treat each other like this! This is not acceptable!"

Almost like they had premeditatively practiced it, both girls burst into tears. Malachi leaned his head back upon his shoulders and wanted to be anywhere else than where he was at. Both girls were now wailing and looking at their father as if he had taken a meager morsel of food from a starving person.

Abruptly, the front door opened and Lisa cheerfully announced, "I'm home."

In unity, the frantic girls ran to their mother and through heaving sobs mumbled, "Mom, Dad is screaming at us."

Lisa shot a surprised look toward Malachi. "Honey, is everything all right?"

Malachi was not happy with Lisa's look and felt he was being judged because of the theatrics of the young ladies. "No, everything is not all right. Your daughters have been fighting since we've been home from school and I've not been able to do any studying. You know I have a big test this Friday."

Lisa was being mobbed by four little hands tightly wrapped around her and the girls were peering back at their father with disgust at his audacity to raise his voice at them. The sympathetic deliberation of the girls fueled a fire inside Malachi and he spouted, "And another thing, you've been letting them get away with too much lately."

Now it was Lisa's turn to become defensive and with her eyebrows arched stated, "I have been letting them get away with too much? So now it's my fault that you are screaming at the girls?"

Malachi tried to back down. "I have not been screaming at the girls."

But at that remark, both girls adamantly shook their heads and joined forces, "Yes, Mom, he has been mean to us."

Lisa inquisitively looked at Malachi. "Are you being mean to the girls?"

Malachi threw his hands up in the air and stomped off. "I'm going to the library. Maybe I can have some peace and quiet there."

Lisa tried to look into his eyes as he brushed by the huddled mass but Malachi's frustration blinded him.

Four hours later, Lisa heard the sound of the garage door opening and knew that Malachi would soon be walking through the door. After his hurried departure, she calmed the girls and explained to them how they were supposed to be helping Dad when he was studying.

The grouping of girls then ate a hastily thrown together dinner of chicken nuggets and watched a sappy sitcom aimed at preteens on Nickelodeon. The girls laughed along with the prearranged laugh track but Lisa was preoccupied thinking about Malachi and how, even her day had not gone well, as a customer rudely argued about a past due bill.

Then it was bath time and bedside prayers and a common refrain included in both sets of Heavenly directed utterances were, "And help Dad." Lisa found this addition mildly amusing but also wondered if she should be praying in this manner as well.

After shedding the work clothes she had been wearing all day, Lisa climbed into comfortable pajamas and was leaning back on their brown suede recliner. Malachi came into the living room. "Are the girls in bed?"

"Yes, they are honey, Are you all right?"

Malachi's chest expanded as he breathed in deeply. "Sure."

But the resigned way Malachi said, "Sure," didn't convince Lisa he was all right, "No, honey, I mean it, you seem a little on edge."

"I'm on edge? Maybe it's because the girls can't get along for two minutes? Maybe it's because I have to work at school all day? Maybe it's because I have one of my biggest and hardest tests this week and three days a week I have to do all the work at home . . . "

"Honey, we talked about me going back to work. We talked about how there would be times when getting your master's would be hard too."

"It shouldn't be this hard."

Lisa, trying to lighten Malachi's mood with humor. "Oh come on, you're tougher than two little girls."

Malachi was not in a joking mood and snapped, "Oh, those two little girls? The ones who you always take their side when they complain about mean old Dad?"

"Honey, I don't always take their side."

"Oh, it sure seemed like it tonight," and he mockingly repeated Lisa's comment about him being 'mean to the girls.'"

Lisa, wanting to deescalate Malachi from working himself up. "Honey, I was just a little surprised about what was going on. I had a terrible day at work and when I just come through the door, there is a lot of crying and . . . "

Malachi raised his voice. "Oh so your day was terrible? But what happens when I have a bad day?"

Lisa stood and took a defensive posture. "So, are you going to scream at me like you have been screaming at the girls?"

"Well, I guess I'm just a terrible father."

"Honey, I've never said that."

But Malachi was starting a downhill descent and held his hands up indicating for her not to come closer. "No, but I'm sure you think I'm a terrible husband."

"Malachi Edward, I don't know what's going on in your head right now but you are not a terrible husband. I'm really not quite sure what's going on but I have never said anything like that."

Malachi should have stopped digging since he was opening a deep hole. "You may not have said it, but I can tell it's how you feel. And another thing, only my mother can call me Malachi Edward."

Lisa's eyes flared with anger and she sarcastically remarked, "Oh, only your mother? Well how do you think she would feel if she knew you were treating your wife this way?"

Malachi allowed the vicious thought that ran through his head that he should not have allowed out of his mouth to come out. "I knew it. You've always been jealous because of the phone calls from Heaven. You resent the fact that I get to talk to Mom every five years."

With large tears forming in her eyes, Lisa was incredulous and folded her arms tightly across her chest. "I can't believe you just said that."

Malachi, knowing he should be quiet, knowing he wounded his wife, knowing that he didn't really mean the hurtful venom that just spewed from his mouth, continued, "And I know that you're mad because you had to go back to work. If I made more money, you could be at home with the girls."

At this point, Lisa was openly weeping as she retreated back onto the recliner and curled up into a little ball. "Honey, I'm sorry, I don't know what's going on with us."

A tiny sliver of regret creeped into Malachi's mind. "I guess I'm sorry too. I'm going to bed." Then he turned and slinked back to their bedroom alone.

For a long time, Lisa wiped the streams of moisture away from her cheeks and was crushed. She knew her husband was frustrated but she didn't know how to help him. She knew they had many things taking place in their lives but didn't everyone? Lisa continued to tighten the grip around herself hoping that tonight had never happened.

Malachi had a difficult time going to sleep and knew he should rush into the living room and profusely apologize to his wife but rationalized excuses why he wouldn't do the right thing. He finally was able to slip into slumber a couple of hours later but then was awakened by Lisa as she was trying to quietly climb into bed and not disturb him.

As his eyes opened, Malachi thought, "It's a good thing I didn't apologize. Look how inconsiderate she's being. Waking me up like this."

The once normal healthy relationship Malachi and Lisa shared seemed to be a distant memory for the next few days. Their conversations were brief and appeared almost professional as if they were a team of workers supplying information to each other during a shift change.

A few times, Lisa wanted to run to her husband and embrace him and make all this go away but Malachi's standoffish demeanor gave her great caution. They had been married for almost eighteen years and encountered the regular challenges and ups and downs of married life but now, Lisa felt as if they were standing on opposite sides of a huge ravine with no way of coming together.

The week slowly ticked away and Malachi took the test. He didn't fare as well as he had on other tests but it was still a decent grade. The girls continued to fight and then make up and then fight and then make up. Customers at Lisa's work were still arguing about their invoices and a dreary routine of mediocrity settled over the house.

It was now a week before Malachi's forty-first birthday and Lisa was hoping the phone call from his mother might be the event that allowed them to bounce back into everything being all right. One night after the girls were soundly sleeping, Lisa mentioned to Malachi, "Honey, your birthday is coming up soon. What if you and I went away from a couple of days? Just you and me? We can get your father and Tina to watch the kids, it'd be good."

Malachi smiled but it seemed contrived and fake. "That would be nice but you know that we really can't afford it. Plus, another birthday is really not that big a deal."

Lisa tried to hide her hurt but knew it was evident as her facial expression was overcome with a still sadness. "O.K., but if you change your mind, please let me know."

Again, Malachi flashed a frozen smile that Lisa knew was only an act. "I will honey, thanks."

The day of Malachi's birthday arrived and Lisa took the day off work and was going to pick the girls up from school and meet Malachi at his favorite restaurant, Texas Roadhouse, later that evening to celebrate his birthday. Lisa was hoping he had a good day and his phone call with Karen would help him.

Malachi arranged to take personal time away from school on the afternoon of his birthday and decided to walk around Edgewater park by himself. He was looking forward to talking to his mother but since he and Lisa were not connecting, he was out of sorts.

Malachi's body posture stiffened when he realized he was passing by the weather-beaten wooden picnic table that he proposed to Lisa years ago. A sly smile crossed his face and he lowered his head as he thought, "For better or worse, 'til death do us part." Slowly, Malachi sauntered over to the table and sat down on it remembering the joy and love he felt when he proposed to Lisa.

Malachi's thoughts were jarred when his phone came to life. He completely forgotten the time. It was 1:17 p.m. When Malachi saw the word Heaven, he almost burst into tears. He wasn't sure if they were tears of joy at being able to talk to his mother or tears of sorrow due to how he was getting along with his wife. Either way, he slid the green talk button over and heard words that caused his heart to race every five years.

"Happy Birthday, my beautiful gift from God!"

"Mom, it's so good to hear your voice."

"It is wonderful to hear your voice."

"Mom, I just really needed to talk to you today."

"Is everything all right honey?"

Malachi flashed back to when Lisa asked him if everything was all right but that query felt much more different coming from his mother. "I just have a lot going on now."

"What's going on honey? Is everyone O.K.?"

Malachi almost laughed out loud as he thought about the family confrontation in the hallway. "Oh yea, everything's great. Just normal stuff."

"What do you mean?"

"Oh, Mom, we don't get to talk a lot. It's just life. I'm overwhelmed, it's nothing big."

"Honey, what's going on?"

It was as if Malachi couldn't hold back any longer. "Mom, my life is a mess. Kids at school are acting up. I'm taking classes for my master's degree and it's much harder than I imagined. The girls are constantly fighting."

"Honey, I'm so sorry that you are hurting. How is Lisa?"

Malachi began weeping. "Mom, we're not getting along. It seems like every time we turn around, we get into a fight. I know there are times when I'm being a jerk to her but I just can't help it. I don't know what to do."

"Honey, welcome to marriage."

Malachi was almost put off by her seemingly dismissal of his feelings. "What do you mean, Mom? I'm telling you we're having serious problems and you're telling me it's not a big deal?"

"Of course, it's a big deal. You and Lisa are having a rough time. That's normal. We all have rough patches in our relationships. There were times your father and I didn't see eye to eye."

Malachi was a little stunned at that comment. "Really? I never saw you and Dad having problems."

"Honey, there was never a time that I didn't love your father but there were times when I didn't like him very much."

"What? I thought you two had a wonderful marriage?"

"Honey, we did. We had a beautiful and healthy marriage but there are times when you're together on the mountain top and everything is delightful and times when you are crawling in the valley when everything is miserable. And during the times in the valley, you don't always feel like you're crawling the same direction."

"Mom really, I never knew you and Dad had struggles."

"We had seasons of trials."

"But Mom, I didn't know you had a bad marriage."

"Oh no, no, honey, your father and I didn't have a bad marriage. We had a fantastic one! But it was a normal one and even the best marriages are not immune to troubles."

"Mom, I had no idea."

Karen launched into a mother/son teaching moment. "Honey, do you remember when you were twelve years old and you stayed with Grandma and Grandpa because Mom and Dad took a trip for a few days?"

Malachi's thoughts raced back through his memory banks. "Yes, I think I remember."

"Your father and I didn't go on a vacation. We went to a marriage conference on how to work on our relationship problems."

Malachi found himself actually raising his left hand in a stopping motion. "Hold on Mom. You and Dad had to go to a marriage conference about relationship problems?"

"Yes, honey, that's what I said."

Malachi felt as if a new discovery was opening up and he wasn't sure if he wanted to know about it. "What happened? What was going on that you two had problems?"

"We were just drifting apart a little. Your father and I always had a healthy, vibrant relationship but then he became more involved at school. I wasn't working outside the home anymore. You were a preteen who could be a headache."

"I know what it's like to have a preteen who can be a headache."

"Hey, be nice to my granddaughter. Besides, she's just like you at that age."

"I guess I received the mother's curse, to have a child act just like I acted." And they both laughed.

"It gets better, I promise. The next few years with the girls may be a little dramatic but they pass so quickly. Please enjoy them."

Malachi knew his mother was speaking into his life. "I know Mom. I guess I'm so frustrated. I thought when I got into my forties that I would have everything together."

"Honey, you're not going to have everything together until you get to Heaven with us."

"Heaven, is that what Heaven is all about? When everything comes together?"

"That's exactly what Heaven is all about. Here there is only peace and joy and contentment . . . "

"But aren't you sad hearing that Lisa and I are having problems?"

Karen tenderly corrected him. "Honey, you and Lisa are just experiencing life. Now what you do with it will either draw you closer or push you farther apart."

"Farther apart. I'm afraid that's what's happening now. I feel so far away from my wife."

Karen offered practical advice. "Honey, the good thing about feeling so far away from her is that you can run back to her."

"Mom, I really have been a jerk lately. I don't know what's going on in my head."

"Honey, so what is exactly going on?"

"Mom, I don't know. I love teaching but sometimes I don't know if I'm making a difference. At times I don't know why I'm trying to get another degree. I don't always know if I'm a good father. I don't even know if I'm a good husband. I mean, look Mom, my wife has to work because we need the money." Malachi was not sure if he felt better or worse after all this spilled from his soul.

"Honey, welcome to being human."

Malachi leaned back a little on the table. "Oh, at first, you welcomed me to marriage and now to being human?"

"Honey, what you are experiencing is life and life is hard. When you endure and overcome the challenges on earth, it makes Heaven even more incredible."

It started to sink into Malachi's mind but more importantly, his heart. "So life on earth is just setting us up to experience and enjoy God's goodness forever?"

"Yes, and of course, God is good to us on earth as well but it's only a glimpse of His goodness and greatness."

Malachi, once again, found himself blown away at the thought of Heaven. "Mom, again when you talk about Heaven all I can think of is wow."

"Honey when you get here you will experience more wow than you can comprehend."

"Is more wow a theological term they teach you up in Heaven?"

"You will learn more up here that will make you think that wow is dull."

A small sense of peace started moving through Malachi's soul. "Mom, for the first time in a long time, I really believe that everything is going to be all right."

"That's what I'm trying to teach you. Yes, everything is going to be all right. The girls will be all right. You and Lisa will be all right. Just make sure that you and the Father are all right."

Malachi felt a twinge of conviction. "I've not been where I should be with God. I've not rejected Him, Mom but I should be closer to Him."

"I know honey," Karen said in almost a whisper.

"Well Mom, I'm going to do something about that. I've been blessed by the Father in so many ways. I have a job that I love. I have a beautiful family. I have an incredible wife. I really do have so much." Malachi's heart felt a heaviness being lifted away from it.

"Honey, our time is almost up."

Malachi wanted more time with his mother. "Mom, I really needed this call. I really needed your help."

"Honey, it's not about me. Turn to the Father and He'll help you through the tough times on earth."

Malachi's spirit was elevated and he felt lighter and heard familiar words that both bothered him and encouraged him, "Never forget that I love you with all of my heart." Then the phone went silent.

Malachi rocked back and forth upon the stiff edge of the solid picnic table that was now being transformed into a sanctuary of holy ground. Legions of powerful heavenly forces surrounded him. Malachi was being ushered into a rare state of Heaven and earth intersecting together.

It had been too long but Malachi found himself talking to the Father and thanking Him for how good He's been to him. Malachi begged forgiveness from the Father for taking it all for granted. But most of all, Malachi rededicated himself to the Father and experienced a renewal and joy that consumed him.

Malachi felt like a new creation. He wasn't the same man that plopped down onto the battered picnic table. He knew he had to rush to find his family and tell them how much he loved them and how sorry he was for not being the man of God he should be for them.

He also knew that somewhere in Heaven his mother was smiling from ear to ear.

# *Eight*

MALACHI reached into his shirt pocket to retrieve his phone to call Lisa. His heart was racing as each successive ring lasted forever. Finally, Malachi was overcome with joy and a huge smile erupted on his face as he heard her response, "Hello, birthday boy."

"Honey, where are you?" Malachi blurted out almost as fast as streams of water frantically gushing out of a red fire hydrant sitting on a city street corner.

"I'm at home. I'm going to get the girls in about an hour . . . "

Malachi didn't mean to cut her off but wanted so much to see her. "Good, that leaves us with a little bit of time. I'll see you in a few minutes."

"O.K., are you all right? We were going to leave you alone this afternoon and meet you later at the restaurant."

Malachi had pulled out of the parking lot and heading east toward home. "I know but I just want to see you now."

"I'm home. See you in a couple of minutes. Bye." Perplexed, Lisa hung up the phone after Malachi echoed her last word and started thinking how she wasn't sure how to take that verbal exchange.

Lately, Malachi was dealing with so much stress that it had grown into a gigantic mountain between them, pushing them apart. She caught herself occasionally blaming herself for their situation but couldn't come up with a different plan to help them get better.

Lisa then started wondering, "Do I jump up and hug him when he gets home?" But then other thoughts flooded her mind, "Or do I brace myself for another fight?"

Contradicting views raced through Lisa's mind so she took a deep breath and let out a small prayer. "Father, help Malachi and me. I'm not sure what's going on."

Almost if on cue, when Lisa opened her eyes from her short jot to God, the door opened and Malachi charged toward Lisa. At first, she didn't know if she should hastily retreat to safety but the loving look upon his face convinced her to stay seated on their leather recliner.

Walking with arms outstretched, Malachi knelt down on the floor in front of the padded recliner and closed his arms around his stunned wife. "I'm so sorry. I've been such a jerk. I love you more than anything. I've been so focused on what's going on with me that I've neglected you and the girls. Please forgive me."

Lisa's eyes burst wide open and before she could utter a word, Malachi continued, "And another thing, you and the girls are the best thing that God could have ever given to a man. I've taken you for granted and I'm so sorry I've not been the husband and father that I should be."

Lisa's eyes swelled. "Honey, I'm sorry too but you are a wonderful father and the greatest husband."

Malachi snuggled his head upon her lap. "I haven't been that wonderful lately."

"Not lately but usually you are." And both their chests heaved with laughter.

Malachi leaned back away from the recliner and sweetly pulled Lisa toward him on the carpeted floor. While being whisked from her seated position, Lisa yelped, "Oh my, be careful. We haven't rolled on the floor for a while."

"I know and I have missed it."

Now they were both sprawled out together with Lisa laying on top of her husband. "And I've missed my husband."

"He's back and the other one is gone."

"Good! I was about to exchange that other one for this one right here."

Playfully shifting to face each other, with his eyebrows uplifted, Malachi answered, "Well this one is the one who is going to stay." As he leaned in he kissed his wife.

Lisa was not wanting to interrupt their sweet reconciliation but curiosity was growing in her mind. "So what's going on? Why the change of heart?"

Malachi again tenderly kissed his bride. "You know, I talked with my mother and she told me that sometimes there are tough times in marriage. And yes, I remember when we were arguing and you asked, 'What would my mother think about how I am treating you?'"

A smirk grew upon Lisa's face, not a smug one but one of joy knowing her husband was back.

"Besides, I know how you women stick together."

Lisa cocked her head to the side. "Oh you do, do you? What exactly did your mother say to you?"

Malachi rested his head closer to her. "She told me that even her and dad had challenges. Did you know when I was twelve, they went to a marriage retreat because they were having problems? Of course, you didn't know. I didn't even know. I just thought they went on a vacation. Anyway, Lisa, I love you with all of my heart and please keep loving me."

Lisa passionately lunged forward. "I will always love you. Don't ever forget that."

Malachi, seductively winked. "How much time do we have before we have to get the girls?"

Lisa plopped a sweet, lingering kiss upon his lips. "Not enough, but later we'll celebrate your birthday." After this promise, Lisa placed her hands on the floor to push herself up.

Malachi shifted to a seated position. "I'll hold you to that birthday gift."

"I know you will. Now I have to go get the girls. You know what'll happen if I'm late. I'll hear it from your oldest daughter."

Malachi reached out his hand toward her for her to help him up. "Yes, she definitely will let you know what she's thinking."

Clasping his hand, Lisa tugged Malachi into a standing position and once again, he wrapped his arms around her in a charming embrace. "What are you going to do now, honey? We planned on meeting you later at the restaurant."

Malachi removed his hands from around Lisa and lifted them in the air with his palms straight up. "I'm going with you to get the girls and this birthday we're not going to Texas Roadhouse. We're going to Chuck E. Cheese."

"Chuck E. Cheese? For your birthday?"

"It'll be good for the girls to have some fun with their dad."

"Yes, it would. Let's go."

"Are you sure we don't have a little more time before we have to get them."

Lisa dodged his roving hands as he affectionately pawed at her. "Later and don't worry, I will make it worth your wait."

Malachi twisted his head in a swooning motion. "First, Chuck E. Cheese and then time with my wife, life doesn't get any better than this!"

Opening the closet door to get her coat, Lisa commented, "And don't ever forget it."

Raising his hand to his brow to salute her as if she were a superior officer, Malachi beamed, "I never will."

As they pulled into the caravan of minivans, SUVs, and cars lined up to pick up their children, Malachi turned to Lisa, "Let me tell the girls about Chuck E. Cheese please."

"Oh, don't worry about that. This is your birthday."

As they inched forward, Malachi could see the girls standing next to the teacher's aide holding a squawking walky-talky telling the teachers which child to bring out of the school building next to be picked up. Once they saw him, they started jumping up and down in excitement. Finally, the car arrived at the loading spot and the girls rushed toward it.

Opening the back door, both girls exuberantly jumped into the car. "Daddy, Daddy. We didn't think we were going to see you until later tonight!"

Malachi turned toward them and reached back and tickled each girl. "I know but we're not going to Texas Roadhouse tonight."

Donna quickly frowned. "We're not going to eat out? But it's your birthday."

Kimberly pulled back and folded her arms demonstrating that she was joining the mini revolution. "How come Dad?"

"Because we are going somewhere different. We are going to Chuck E. Cheese!"

Both girls erupted with joy. "Chuck E. Cheese! This will be the best birthday ever!"

Lisa turned toward the girls. "Yes, we are going to have fun but first buckle up."

As the small Byrge entourage filed out of the passenger picking up line, merriment filled the car and Lisa issued instructions. "We are going home to change out of our school clothes and then we can go."

Again, squeals of pleasure were emitted from the girls and Malachi. As they pulled onto their concrete driveway, Malachi quickly pushed his car door open and waited to give both girls one of the biggest hugs of their lives.

As Malachi was enveloping the girls in his arms, he said, "Girls, lately Dad has had a lot going on and I'm sorry I haven't been myself so we're going to go have some fun. I love you two with all of my heart."

With both girls jumping up and down in his embrace, Lisa looked over and huge smile crossed her face. Donna stated, "Dad, we love you too but let go of us so we can get out of our school clothes and get there."

Kimberly too chimed in as Malachi was smothering them with kisses, "Dad, we have to go. Chuck E. Cheese is waiting."

With all of the huddled excitement taking place, Lisa walked to the front door, unlocked it, and held it open while two whirl-winds of energy released from their father's arms dashed toward their rooms to change. Lisa raised her hand to her mouth and called out, "Don't just throw your clothes on the ground girls. Please put them in your hampers."

The girls didn't take too long and soon they were buckled into the backseat already planning what games they were going to play at Chuck E. Cheese. In the bell whirring, buzzer chiming, bright lights flashing, stampeding kids running loose, place of pandemonium, Malachi and the girls went from game to game collecting rows of perforated tickets to exchange later for coveted prizes.

After floppy slices of pepperoni pizza, garlic bread sticks dipped in mozzarella sauce, loads of soda, and hands full of plastic prizes selected from the glass counter smudged with hundreds of tiny fingerprints, the Byrges loaded back into their van.

Donna, tried to suppress a yawn, "That was the best birthday ever!"

Kimberly echoed her agreement, "That was the bestest birthday!"

Malachi looked back the girls in the rearview mirror and then glanced at Lisa, "That was the bestest birthday ever!"

The next five years passed by so rapidly that both Malachi and Lisa felt they couldn't keep up. Both girls were teenagers, which was a brand-new experience for their parents who were in a state of constant confusion when dealing with them. Malachi received his master's degree and when he strolled across the elevated stage in his black robe, he paused and looked out at his family clapping and shouting, "Yea, Dad."

Stiffly, Malachi rolled out of bed on his forty-sixth birthday. Slowly rubbing his shoulder as he rotated it, he thought about how many people teased him about getting older. While forty-six is not that old, it is not that young either. Malachi slowly walked to the bathroom to take a shower and reflected how fast life progresses.

At school, Malachi's day was planned as he had a teacher in service day where he and his colleagues were expected to watch an online lecture and catch up on their grades and progress reports. Malachi previously cleared that afternoon of all appointments so he could receive the anticipated phone call from Heaven.

The videoed lecture was informative but Malachi found himself lifting his eyes toward the round, ticking clock mounted on the wall of his classroom more and more as the afternoon was approaching. With his desk cleared, Malachi placed his phone on his rectangular daily calendar and knew the call was close.

Malachi's head jerked up toward the clock as his phone came to life. It was 1:17 p.m. With a grin spreading upon his face, he slid the talk button over to the right.

"Happy Birthday, my beautiful gift from God."

"Mom, it's so good to hear you."

"Honey, it's so good to hear you too. So what's happening? What's going on in your life? How are the girls? How is Lisa? You are still with Lisa, right?"

Malachi feigned shock. "Mom, of course I'm with Lisa!"

"Oh, I know honey. I was just teasing."

"Of course you know and also, you should know that things are well with us."

"Honey, I'm so glad things are good for you and Lisa."

"Mom, things started getting much better after you and I talked five years ago. I was really being selfish and needed you to help me understand that you have to work at marriage."

"Honey, I'm so happy for you and yes, there are times when marriage can be tough but you and Lisa love each other and will work everything out. How was your birthday party five years ago?"

Malachi rested back into his chair. "Oh Mom, you have no idea. Instead of going to our normal place we went to Chuck E. Cheese and had the greatest time."

"You had the bestest birthday ever!"

Malachi slowly shook his head. "Mom, I always forget that you're able to have glimpses of our life when we're having good times."

"I wish I had been there with the girls because you all had so much fun."

Malachi leaned back over his desk with a smile on his face. "Yes, we did. But I'm not sure if the girls would have such a good time now at Chuck E. Cheese. You know they are both teenagers now."

"Teenage daughters, now the real fun will begin."

"Oh, don't worry, we've already had a few knockdown drag out discussions about what we expect and how things are going to be."

"And you will have many more discussions in the near future. I remember there were times when you tested your father and me. We would lay down the law and sometimes you obeyed it, sometimes you walked right to the edge of it, and there were times when sometimes you defiantly ran right past that line."

"What? Mom, I'm sure I was the perfect teenager."

"Don't you believe that, dear."

Malachi started to say how tough it was to be sixteen since that was how old Donna was now but then caught himself. Karen picked up on it and replied, "Honey, did you stop talking about Donna being sixteen because that's how old you were when I came to Heaven?"

Malachi wasn't sure how to respond. "Mom, I didn't want to bring up any bad memories."

"Oh honey, coming to Heaven is not a bad memory in any way. I do miss spending more time with you and your father but being here and being able to see when things are good for you is wonderful."

"Mom, do these phone calls make you sad?"

"No, they don't make me sad. It's hard to explain. I miss you all and I miss being away and not experiencing the good times with you all but being in the presence of the Father is more satisfying than anything you could ever comprehend."

Malachi had a burning question that had rummaged through his mind for many years but was afraid to ask his mother. "Mom, I have a silly question and I don't mean anything bad but do you ever get bored in Heaven?"

"Bored? What do you mean bored?"

Malachi felt he was being heretical. "I mean you do the same thing every day, all the time, right?"

"I see what you are asking now. No honey, we're never bored in Heaven. The Father is so big that every time we turn around, we learn something more of Him. Every time we worship Him He gets bigger and greater and His love for us saturates through every ounce of our being. Plus, there is no time in Heaven, it's just eternal peace and joy."

"Mom, I've really tried to understand Heaven but I guess I don't get it."

"And that's O.K. honey, do you remember the account in Revelation where the Heavenly creatures are crying out, 'Holy, holy, holy'?"

Malachi was trying to picture the creatures in his mind. "Yes Mom, what exactly do they look like?

"It wouldn't make a difference if I tried to explain it because you wouldn't be able to understand. But anyway, they are praising the Father by saying 'Holy, holy, holy' because every time they turn around, they're astounded at His power and what He's doing."

"God is still working in Heaven?"

"Oh yes, the Father is loving us and taking care of all you on earth."

With Malachi's free hand, he ran his fingers through his brown, slightly graying hair. "Mom, I'm really blown away. Heaven sounds like something so incredible that I'll never figure it out."

"Exactly! We'll be amazed by the Father for all eternity. That's why we are not bored. But I think someone as smart as my son would be able to figure it all out."

"What do you mean as smart as I am?"

"You have your master's degree now and I'm so proud of you."

"Thanks Mom, but it really is no big deal."

"Malachi Edward, it is a big deal that you earned your degree. You worked hard for it and I know your father was very proud and I am too."

"Thanks Mom."

"Honey, there are a couple of important things that we have to talk about."

Malachi shifted his weight back in his chair and took a deep breath as if he were anticipating hearing something hard. "O.K., Mom. You sound serious. Is everything all right?"

"Of course, it is well but our phone calls are going to be changing."

"What do you mean, Mom? Are we still going to be able to talk every five years? Is there a problem?"

Karen sensed Malachi was growing concerned. "No, there's not a problem. The Father gave us this incredible gift thirty years ago because when I came to Heaven, it was very difficult for you."

"Difficult, that's an understatement."

Karen could hear the mounting tension in her son's voice. "Yes, it was but the Father wanted you to know how good He is and also wanted to give me this special gift."

"Our phone calls have been a gift to you too?"

"Oh honey, more than you know. But the Father and I've been talking and He knows that you're solid and don't need my encouragement as much as you have before . . . "

Malachi interrupted his mother. "Mom, I have so much more to learn from you. I have so many more questions about Heaven."

"That's true but the questions of Heaven will be answered when you arrive. So, the Father has granted us two more phone calls."

"We can only talk two more times?"

Karen was trying to calm the anxiety growing in Malachi's spirit. "Yes, and it will be every ten years. The first one will be when you turn 56 years old and our last phone call will be when you are 66 years old. We will have talked for fifty years since I came to Heaven."

"But Mom, it's not fair. I'm used to your calls every five years."

Karen gently rebuked him. "Malachi, so many sons never received a phone call from a parent who came to Heaven so don't ever think that the new plan is not fair."

Shame slowly crept through Malachi's heart. "Mom, you're right. Please tell the Father that I'm sorry for being upset about only having two more phone calls from you. I know that this was a unique and incredible gift."

"Honey, He forgives you and understands how you're feeling."

Malachi then felt he was bombarded with a barrage of questions. "So will our last two calls be on my birthday at 1:17 p.m.?"

"Yes and remember how quickly every five years has gone. You are now at an age where every ten years will pass just as quickly."

Malachi leaned back again in the chair and thought about the growing amount of aches and pains he was now feeling. "I know that Mom. I'm learning that I'm not twenty years old anymore."

"Honey, you have not been twenty years old for a while."

"Please tell the Father that I'm very thankful for the phone calls and I appreciate we have two more."

"He knows."

But then a random thought exploded in Malachi's mind. "But Mom, I just thought something and I'm not sure if I can ask you this or not."

"Go ahead and if I can answer you I will and if not, I'll let you know."

Malachi wasn't sure if he wanted to vocalize the nagging thought in his mind. "Mom, if we are not going to talk after I turn 66 years old, am I going to die then?"

"Honey, don't even worry about that. It will all make sense in time. I can't tell you when you're coming to Heaven but it won't be for a while."

Malachi felt a sense of relief but then felt bad. "Mom, I don't mean that I don't want to come to Heaven to see you and David and all of our other family. I just . . . "

"I understand honey, you are all right."

Malachi breathed a sigh of relief. "Thanks Mom."

"There is one more thing that I asked the Father's permission to share with you during this phone call."

Malachi, again felt his pulse racing and his stomach churning. "What is it Mom?"

"Spend some extra time with your father."

Malachi's eyes shot open in a circled reflex. "Dad? Why is something going to happen to Dad? Is Dad going to Heaven?"

"Honey, we want everyone to come to Heaven and I can't tell you any more than that. Just spend some time with Dad."

Malachi was trying to process this earthshattering piece of information and a numbness seemed to settle over him. "Mom, thanks for telling me."

"Honey, if there is any part of our phone calls that are hard for me, it is now, but I have to go."

"Mom, I know. I hate when they are over as well."

"Never forget that I love you with all of my heart!"

As the phone line went silent, Malachi sat very still. Even his breathing was measured and he perceived his heart was pumping slower. After all of the phone calls from his mother, he was generally encouraged and excited. But he didn't know how to feel after this one. Rampant emotions such as confusion, sadness, anxiety, uncertainty, and so many other feelings sifted through his soul.

Malachi barely remembered standing up by his large wooden classroom desk and collecting his papers to place into his leather briefcase. During the drive home, Malachi seemed much more introspective about life, how much time he and his father had on earth, and countless inquiries about Heaven.

When he arrived home, he paused before opening the front door and thought, "I don't want to bother Lisa about how I'm feeling but I know she's going to ask how the phone call went."

Pushing the door open, he heard Lisa calling out to Donna about leaving the plate that held her snack of pringles chips on the coffee table and ordering her to take it to the kitchen sink. Donna, responded in a teenage tone, "I was going to get that later, Mom."

Lisa seeing Malachi walk in, rolled her eyes to him in the direction of Donna, "Yes, I know that you were but I appreciate if you did it now."

Donna, grasping the renegade piece of dishware, and storming past her parents, placed it into the sink. "There, now it's done."

Malachi shot her a look of curiosity on why her attitude was so rude but then remembered she was a teenager. As Donna walked to her room, Lisa sided up to Malachi and shifted to a cheerful tone. "How was your phone call?"

Malachi embraced his wife. "I'm not sure."

Lisa's perplexment was obvious as a puzzled look overcame her. "What do you mean, you are not sure?"

Malachi opened their hallway closet door filled with jackets, umbrellas, and a catch all for many other items and placed his briefcase in it. Lisa was watching closely as she wasn't sure what was happening in the mind of her husband. Malachi then went to the living room and plopped down upon one of their padded recliners.

"Are you all right?"

For what seemed to be a long time, Malachi didn't respond. "Yes, every things all right. I just received a couple of interesting comments from Mom."

Lisa moved Malachi's hands that were folded together on his lap and climbed upon his lap. "What do you mean, interesting?"

Malachi seemed to snap out of an opaque fog and gazed directly into his wife's blue eyes. "Mom is only going to call every ten years and only two more times."

"But why, is there anything wrong?"

"No, the Father thinks I'm solid and don't need the phone calls like I once did."

Lisa wrapped her arms around her husband and snuggled in closer to him. "Well, that's true, you are a tremendous man of God. But I know how much the phone calls mean to you."

Malachi smiled and locked his hands around his wife. "Yea, they mean a lot but I'm thankful that they even happened."

"Yes, they were an incredible gift. I'm happy that you are looking at them that way."

Malachi drew her closer.

Lisa's body then bristled. "Wait! If there are only two more calls and will take place every ten years, that doesn't mean that you'll be dead when you turn 66 years old? Does it?"

Malachi shifted his weight to tighten his embrace and snickered. "That's what I asked Mom."

"Well? What did she say?"

Mischievously Malachi lowered his gaze and then his eyes shot back up to his nervous wife. "She said it doesn't mean anything. When I am 66 I will have been blessed with fifty years of phone calls from Heaven."

Lisa sighed a breath of relief but didn't allow herself to completely relax. "You said there were a couple of interesting things she told you."

"She said to spend some extra time with Dad."

"Oh no! Does that mean that Dad won't be with us much longer? Is he going to Heaven soon?"

"I hope not very soon but I should pay attention to what I was told."

As Malachi and Lisa continued to look at each other, Kimberly walked past the living room and smirked, "Would you two quit it? I need someone to take me to soccer practice."

"What, quit this?" And he pulled Lisa closer into him.

Lisa giggled and squirmed out of his arms. "All right lover boy, the taxi service is needed again. Off to soccer."

Malachi reluctantly let go of his wife, separating his arms widely and dropping them off the side of the recliner. "I guess we're done cuddling now."

Lisa leaned forward, gave him a peck on his lips. "Honey, dinner is on the stove and we'll be back in about an hour."

It was amazing how busy and fast paced their lives were with the girls involved in band and soccer and softball. There were also many trips dropping them off and picking them up from the mall where other teenagers leisurely connected together in young angst. Malachi did think back to his conversation with his mother about how time continues to speed up the older you get.

Then he felt a pressing urge to call his father.

# *Nine*

"Hello."

"Dad, how are you? Are you O.K.?"

"Hi, son. Tina, it's Malachi. I'm fine. What's going on?"

Malachi wasn't quite sure how to proceed. He knew he couldn't just spit out that his mother in Heaven told him to spend extra time with him as he pondered how that might be taken. So, he casually remarked, "Oh, not much. The girls and Lisa are good. We're just really busy lately."

"That's good. I'm glad everyone is well. How are you doing? Your voice sounds a little different. Is everything all right?"

"Yea Dad, I'm fine. Everything's good. I was just wondering if you're doing O.K.?"

"That's the second time you've asked me if I am doing O.K. Is there anything I should know?"

Malachi reached up with his left hand and rubbed his wrinkled forehead. "No, Dad. No. I've just been thinking about you." And Malachi's face crinkled as he wondered if he had just been untruthful.

"I'm happy you're thinking about me. Things are good but lately I've been feeling a little more tired than usual."

"What do you mean, more tired than usual? Are you hurting anywhere?"

"I'm really not hurting but let's just put it this way, I'm in my 60's now so I can't be expected to have the energy when I was younger."

"And you're not 20 years old anymore either, old man."

Malachi laughed as he remembered his mother just told him the same thing. "I know Dad, trust me, I feel my age."

"Wait until you get in your 60's."

"I'll be there before I know it."

"Yes, you will. That's why you need to enjoy those girls right now."

Malachi appreciated receiving fatherly advice. "I'm trying Dad but the older they get, the dumber it seems I am. Or at least, that's what they think."

"I remember a 17-year-old once telling me I had a lot to learn."

A huge smile spread across Malachi's face. "Yes, and that 17-year-old is now 46 and is not that smart anymore."

Both father and son reviled in their shared astuteness. Malachi continued, "I just wanted to make sure you're feeling all right."

"I'm fine. You don't have to worry about me. That's Tina's job."

"Yes, it is. But hey Dad, before I let you go. I'd like to set up a time every couple of weeks where we get together. It doesn't have to be anything fancy. I just want to spend some time with you."

"I would like that Malachi. Let me know."

Malachi felt good about their exchange after he and his father bid farewell and ended their conversation.

The next couple of years, Mike and Malachi met at least every two weeks and their bond cemented into an unbreakable foundation. Malachi found himself being amazed at his father as Mike shared feelings and insight that Malachi had never heard. Malachi also appreciated his father's advice in handling teenagers.

Malachi tightly squeezed Lisa's hand while their firstborn daughter, Donna, raised her fist in the air triumphantly as she walked across the elevated stage to receive her high school diploma. As they released their hands to begin clapping ecstatically, Malachi looked over a couple of seats and noticed how much older his father seemed to be.

After the long, speech filled, ceremony ended, Malachi and Lisa stood and picked up the small brochure highlighting each student's activity to place into her scrapbook. As they awaited their excited, bouncing daughter, clad in her scarlet robe, Malachi thought about how beautiful Donna was as she was now a young adult.

A couple of years later, Malachi and Lisa found themselves sitting near where they sat previously and witnessed their youngest child, Kimberly, stroll nonchalantly across the wooden platform filled with teachers and the principal. Donna, now in her second year of college at Anderson University, rolled her eyes toward the sky when her sister, raised up the Hawaiian hang loose symbol once she was handed her diploma.

Malachi and Lisa now had two high school graduates and a son, David, in Heaven. On the ride home from the school's crowded auditorium, Malachi looked lovingly at Lisa and thought how good God has been to him to give him so much. From Lisa's peripheral vision, she caught his gaze and reached over to hold his hand. "Are you all right, hon?"

Malachi, choked up, finally was able to sputter, "I am so blessed. With the girls and with you."

A smile lit up on Lisa's face as she pulled his hand toward her face and planted a tender kiss upon it. "We are blessed. I love you so much." Of course, both girls paused from their rapid-fire discussion about who was wearing what and chimed in, "Would you two stop it?" Malachi peered in the rearview mirror and his eyes twinkled, "When you're married to the most beautiful woman in the world, you can't help it."

The heads of both girls tilted back in mock surrender and they quickly resumed their earlier spirited conversation of the fashion faux pas and who looked good and who did not. Later that fall, Kimberly started attending classes at Ball State, the alma mater of her parents. She seriously considered Anderson University but the campus might not have been able to endure the combined force of two Byrge girls.

The month before Malachi's 51st birthday, a sense of moroseness overtook him. He felt lethargic and at times, Lisa had to repeat questions to him. There were moments when he snapped briskly at her and mumbled how he heard what she said the first time but really had not. It was almost as if Malachi stumbled into a thick fog and was unable to find his bearings.

It was not until the day before his birthday that he came to his senses and realized that he was not himself because he wouldn't be talking to his mother this birthday. For the last thirty years, every fifth birthday, he was able to hear the cheerful voice of his mother. But not this birthday.

One evening, Malachi gingerly approached Lisa to apologize. "Honey, I've not been myself lately."

Lisa placed the book she was reading upon her lap. "So, what's going on?"

"For thirty-five years since I've been sixteen years old, I've been able to talk to Mom. This is the first fifth year birthday that we've not . . . " And he grew silent.

Lisa shifted toward him and wrapped her arms around him. "I thought so."

Malachi surprised himself as tears began to stream from his eyes. "And the girls living at college. I miss them."

Lisa pulled back far enough to raise her hand and tenderly wipe the tears from Malachi's face. "You mean you miss all the drama we used to have?"

Malachi looked into his wife's eyes and laughed. "No, I don't miss that but I do miss them. And I miss Mom. And Dad isn't doing well at all since he's been diagnosed with lung cancer."

Lisa tried to force a sweet smile but sadness overtook her eyes and heart as well. "I know hon, we've had a lot going on."

Malachi's lips tightened together in an attempt to smile back at his wife. "Yes, we have but this is life."

"We still have each other."

"Yes, we do. And I'm really going to need you when Dad . . . "

Lisa started caressing his back in a circular motion. "I know hon. It is going to be hard but we'll get through it together."

Malachi and Lisa held each other fondly as they rocked back and forth.

Three years later, they found each other speaking in hushed whispers as they sat next to the white sheet draped hospital bed where Mike was stretched out. Malachi was holding his father's hand while Lisa rested her hand upon his shoulder, gently touching him. Adjusting the starched, sterile bed covering up to under his father's chin, Malachi shook his head at how emaciated and frail his father appeared.

On the other side of the metal railed, framed bed, Tina was holding Mike's other hand and her eyes were swollen from the many tears that had fallen. The quietness was abruptly broken when Donna and Kimberly entered the room like a whirlwind. Donna had picked her sister up from Muncie and they rushed to the hospital.

Malachi warmly acknowledged the girls. "It won't be much longer. Grandpa is going to Heaven soon. If you want to say anything, now is the time."

The girls wrapped an arm around each other's backs and forged together as one sad unit. Donna, through tears blurted, "Grandpa, we love you so much. We're going to miss you."

With Kimberly's free hand, she started to wipe the wetness from both she and her sister's face, "Grandpa, we love you." And then her voice quivered into quietness.

Malachi thought back at how thankful he was that he and Mike had spent so much time together the last few years. Had he not followed his mother's advice, he would've missed out on so much. But Malachi's heart beat with joy that he truly knew he had a wonderful relationship with his father.

Two hours and fifteen minutes later, a younger, caring nurse wearing her glasses on the top of her head came into the room. After placing the metal pronged stethoscope on Mike's chest and briefly listening for what seemed to be an eternity, she sadly shook her head and offered sincere condolences.

The girls had pulled a chair up to the bottom edge of the bed and then exploded into sobs. Tina laid her head over the cold metal bed railing and was audibly weeping. Lisa tightly wrapped her arms around Malachi while she was standing behind him.

But almost an odd surrealness overtook Malachi. He definitely felt sad but no tears were falling. He was stunned but still coherent. The only thought that ran through his shooting mind was that now Dad was in Heaven with Mom.

Malachi didn't want to verbalize this thought because he didn't want to hurt Tina but felt immersed in a peace knowing it. After standing up, Malachi leaned over the lifeless body of his father, kissed his forehead, and devoutly whispered, "Thank you Father for giving me the greatest earthly father."

As Malachi stepped away, still studying the shell that once held his father, Lisa moved forward and slowly rubbed Mike's gaunt face. "Dad, thank you for being so good to your son and his family."

Tina glanced up at Lisa and as their eyes met, she remarked, "He has been so good to all of us."

The girls, holding each other, moved as one, and wrapped themselves around their father, Malachi. He returned their loving embrace and managed to say, "Girls, he's in Heaven now. He's in a perfect place." They nodded their heads and together shifted by where Lisa was standing and leaned over and kissed their grandfather on his cheek.

Later at the funeral service, Malachi couldn't help but to reflect upon his mother's funeral. He had an undeniable peace throughout it because he'd been able to talk to her for the first time on his sixteenth birthday. Now that he was in his mid-50's, he could still recall the tranquility he felt in his soul.

When Pastor Skinner, their new young preacher, pronounced ashes to ashes and dust to dust, Malachi couldn't hold back a huge smile as he pictured his father and mother reunited.

On Sunday, Malachi's 56th birthday, he and Lisa passed by each other trading places in front of the mirror for a final inspection before they ventured to church. Walking toward their car, Lisa reminded Malachi, "Don't forget, everyone is coming over at 5:00 tonight so we can celebrate your birthday."

After Malachi opened the driver's side door, he paused, "Did we invite Tina?"

"Of course, honey. Everyone should be here."

Malachi shook his head in affirmation.

The worship service at the church was wonderful and Pastor Skinner delivered a Biblically sound and relevant message. Even though he was physically present at church, Malachi found his thoughts wandering about whether or not he would receive a phone call from Heaven. His mother told him he would but now things may be different.

As they were pulling out of the Applebee's parking lot after lunch, Lisa rubbed the back of Malachi's head. "It's 12:30, so when we get home I'm going to change and meet Jenny over at Starbucks so you can enjoy your phone call."

"I hope there is a phone call."

"Oh honey, your mother said she would call you on your 56th birthday so I'm sure she will."

Malachi's eyes twinkled in agreement as he looked over at his wife.

Arriving at the house, Lisa bounded toward the bedroom to change into a more casual wardrobe of blue jeans, a white blouse, and brown leather sandals. Malachi decided not to change and leaned back into their overstuffed recliner and shifted his phone back and forth in his hand.

Before Lisa walked out the front door, she entered the living room and placed both hands on the side of her husband's face, gave it a playful squeeze, and joked, "I can't believe I'm married to such an old man." And then she planted a kiss upon his lips.

As she turned, Malachi swatted her behind. "You are not too far behind me."

"Don't ever forget I'm never too far away from you. I love you." Malachi still played with his phone as he heard the front door close and the roar of the car's engine come to life.

Leaning his head back and closing his eyes, Malachi tried to prepare himself. "Now don't be upset if you don't get a call."

However, his mantra of anticipating something bad was halted by the ringing of his cell phone. Malachi quickly raised his head and his heart beat quicker as the caller id flashed, 'Heaven'.

"Happy Birthday my beautiful gift from God!"

Malachi's spirit was relieved and his pulse started returning to normal. "Mom, it is so good to hear your voice."

"It's so good to hear yours as well! How are the girls? How is Lisa? How are you? Are you taking care of yourself?"

"Mom, we are all good. But I do have to ask you a big question."

"I believe I already know what you are going to ask."

Malachi felt an inward tension but had to forge ahead. "Mom, Dad . . . "

"Yes, Dad is here. As a matter of fact, we asked the Father if he could talk to you during this phone call but the Father said no."

"Why would God not want me to talk to Dad too?"

"Honey, it's been too soon."

"But you were able to call me the day after you went to Heaven. It's been a couple of years since Dad went to Heaven."

"You're right, but you were much younger and much needier. The Father told us that hearing your Dad's voice would not help as much as you think it would."

Malachi bristled a little. "I think it would help."

"Malachi, the Father knows us better than we know ourselves so if He thinks it wouldn't be helpful, then it would not be."

Malachi accepted her explanation. "Mom, I know that but it'd be good just to hear Dad one more time."

"Don't worry, he is standing right next to me and David."

"Do you mean he is with his only grandson?"

"Yes and those two are into everything, everywhere."

"What did Dad do when he got to Heaven?"

"He was first embraced by the Lamb and his eyes were so big. He just kept looking around and taking everything in. And then, he saw David and I and he ran to us."

"Then what did he do?"

"Oh, we hugged and hugged. It's so good to see him again."

Malachi paused as he was trying to conjure a mental picture of his father, mother, and son reunited in a perfect place.

"So, we want to know what's going on? What is happening in your life?"

"Mom, so much has happened. Ever since Dad died . . . "

Karen interrupted, "Honey, Dad didn't die . . . "

"I know, I know. He didn't die. He went to Heaven."

"Exactly, we are more alive than we have ever been. And one day, you and Lisa and the girls and my great-grandchildren will be here."

"Whoa Mom, great grandchildren?"

"Well, you know . . . " Karen playfully elongated each word, "since Donna got married a year ago."

"Oh Mom, it was beautiful. But it was also hard. I just couldn't believe that my daughter was getting married."

"And she married such a nice young man. He will treat her very well."

"He better if he knows what's best for him. Besides, he has no idea that I have a spy in Heaven watching."

"I would hardly consider myself a spy. But it is fun to see your lives unfold."

Malachi wanted to return to his mother's earlier comments. "You mentioned something about great grandkids?"

"Malachi, remember in Heaven we're not bound by time like you are on earth."

"That's why you told me to spend some extra time with Dad. You knew that he was going to Heaven, didn't you?"

"Well hopefully, you all are coming to Heaven, right?"

Malachi moved his head in an affirmative motion. "Yes, Mom. We're not perfect but we have a wonderful relationship with God."

"Oh honey, when you do get to Heaven and meet the Father face to face, you will experience a peace that will overwhelm you."

Malachi begged his mother to continue. "Mom, keep going. Especially since you told me how Dad acted when he got to Heaven, what else is going to happen?"

"First a peace that erases all confusion fills every ounce of your being and then you feel a joy that I can't even begin to describe. It's not really a feeling like when you are having a good time, it's more a full joy that everything is perfect. And then . . . "

"So what does God, I mean, the Father look like?"

"He is everything. He is brighter than the sun that hangs in your sky. He is more powerful than any force of nature and definitely anything man could ever create. When you are in His presence, you are filled with awe."

"Mom, I just can't comprehend it!"

"And honey, I'm not even doing the Father justice."

"Wow, wow, wow," was all that Malachi could mutter in amazement.

"In Heaven, we say holy, holy, holy, but wow is good too."

"So when I get there, I will see the Father and then get to see you all like Dad did?"

Karen felt she was starting to overload Malachi. "Honey, don't try to figure it out. Just enjoy your time on earth with your beautiful wife and great girls and now son-in-law. Soon enough you will join us."

"Mom, just one more thing. When am I coming to Heaven? Is it soon? What will happen when I die? I didn't mean to say I would die, I mean before I come to Heaven. Mom, I have so many questions."

"I know you do Honey and they will all be answered when you get here. And quit worrying, you have a lot of living left."

Internally, Malachi breathed a sigh of relief. "Mom, it's not that I don't want to go to Heaven as I definitely want to you see you guys but I just don't know."

"Honey, one of the countless blessings of Heaven is being reunited with your family and loved ones but remember, the greatest, undeniably, most fantastic part of Heaven is spending eternity with the Father, Son, and Holy Spirit."

"You're right Mom."

"Your Dad is laughing next to me and he said that it took him getting to Heaven to hear you say that one of us was right."

"Oh, that's hilarious."

"Oh, that's nothing. In Heaven you'll laugh and be elated more than you've ever been."

Malachi quietly spoke as he quoted scripture. "There is no pain, no death, no mourning."

"Honey, that's right. On earth, when a loved one comes to Heaven, we miss them but if we truly understood how they are in Heaven, it would make a great difference."

Malachi knew their time was short but wanted it to go on and on. "Mom, your phone calls have made such a difference, not only for me but also Lisa and the girls. When we feel sad about you and Dad and David, we think of you being in a perfect place and it really helps."

Malachi could almost feel the arms of his mother wrapping around him. "Honey, don't ever forget, we didn't die. We came to Heaven."

"But Mom, I have to admit that after we talk, I have so many questions but I do have a peace."

"I know honey and our time is coming to an end. I will call you on your 66th birthday."

Malachi felt winded like he was punched in the stomach. "And it will be our last call?"

"Remember, enjoy the many blessings from the Father and know that He's working everything out."

Malachi started shaking his head as he heard loving words that both helped and haunted him. "Never forget that I love you with all my heart."

Then the phone went silent. Malachi had been encouraged by the phone call but was still plagued by so many unanswered doubts and questions. He knew it was futile to try to understand Heaven but found himself spending more time thinking about it since he was getting older.

The seconds of time dissolved into minutes and before Malachi realized it he had been sitting looking at his phone for almost two hours. He was yanked back into reality when he heard the front door of their home open up. "Honey, I'm home."

A sly smile broke out upon Malachi's face as he thought of the word honey and how Lisa and his mother both used it. His amiable introspection was cut short when Lisa came near to him and asked, "How was your phone call?"

He stood and embraced his wife that he loved so much. "It was wonderful and you are never going to believe this. Dad and David were standing right next to her."

Still cradled in his arms, Lisa leaned back a little. "They were standing right next to her? Did you get to talk to your dad?"

"No, I didn't. I wanted to but the Father, I mean God, didn't think it would be good at this time."

"Now why would God not let you?"

"Mom said that it was too soon. You know, maybe it is too soon and if I heard his voice, it would bother me that he's not with us anymore even though it's been a couple of years."

Lisa started walking over to their multi-shelved bookcase to lay her car keys on it. "You might be right but the more I hear about Heaven, the more I'm overwhelmed."

Malachi's eyebrows raised in consensus. "You're not the only one. I think I realized that more in this phone call than in many of the other ones."

Lisa drew near him and playfully poked him in the side. "That's because you are getting older."

Malachi pulled her down to the couch. "Hey Mom said for me to enjoy the blessings that God has given us, so, let's start enjoying."

Giggling, Lisa squirmed from his release. "I have a party to get ready for. It's someone's birthday."

Malachi stuck out his lips in a pouting gesture. "Hmmph, people coming over to remind me I'm getting older. Sounds like a party to me."

"Don't you be a party pooper. Besides your new son-in-law is coming and I've even heard that Kimberly might be bringing a special friend."

"What, not another wedding! We haven't paid this one off yet."

Lisa shot him a wifely look that sent a signal for him to settle down. "Stop it. It was worth every penny."

"Yes, it was. I just don't know if I'm ready for both of my girls to be married."

Lisa directed her pointer finger at her husband. "Slow down, they are just dating. Now, don't embarrass your daughter when they get here."

In a Groucho Marx like manner, Malachi raised his eyebrows up and down. "I would never do that."

Both he and Lisa laughed as she headed to the kitchen.

Malachi sank back upon the couch and thought how happy he was at that very moment. He knew how blessed he was and then started imagining, "If the joy in Heaven is anything like I feel now, it is a perfect place."

# Ten

MALACHI slowly scanned their crowded living room and his heart was filled with peace and joy. A raucous rendition of "Happy Birthday" was vigorously belted out by his energetic family members. His two daughters, Donna, standing next to her husband, Roy, Kimberly with a 'new friend', Tina, and Lisa comprised the conglomeration before him.

Malachi's smile spread broadly across his face and a couple of tears thinly streaked down his cheeks. After the invigorating performance, worthy of any Broadway concert hall, the enthusiastic mob called out, "Make a wish and blow out your candles!"

Donna added, "That's if you can come up with enough breath, old man."

In jest, Kimberly piled on the insults, "If you need our help, Dad, we're right here."

The others joined in the revelry but Malachi's brow furrowed in mock disdain. "Thank you very much. I don't need your help." And he leaned forward and inhaled for an extra-long time as he knew if he didn't blow out all the candles he would be the subject of much mocking and endless teasing.

The tiny flames jutting out of the ends of the wax multi-colored candles flickered as they were systematically extinguished and Malachi leaned back, "Ha, you all didn't have any faith."

Lisa picked up the now smoldering chocolate iced cake and started walking toward the kitchen. "Who wants ice cream with your cake?"

Tina, jumped out her chair, following Lisa, and said, "I'd be happy to help you."

Donna and Kimberly scooped up several presents neatly enveloped in over the hill and gag wrapping paper. Malachi, thrilled by the overwhelming love exuding from his family, quipped, "Oh great, more socks and wallets."

Donna jabbed back, "Don't forget underwear too."

Malachi shot her a playful face as he wiggled his head in feigned disgust. By that time, Lisa and Tina returned balancing circular plates of scrumptious chocolate cake nestled up against a small mountain of delicious French vanilla ice cream saturated with bits and chunks of Oreo cookies. As Malachi received his treat, he gladly dug into his prized delicacy.

After all had been served and a momentary period of silence took place because all were enjoying the sweet dessert, Donna placed her cake stained and ice cream residue plate to the side and stood and said, "I have an announcement."

She looked over at Roy and transmitted a secret look which made him hurriedly put his unfinished dessert on the brown coffee table and quickly stood beside his wife. Donna clasped Roy's hand, "We are going to have a baby!"

Oohs and aahs flooded the room and hugs began to contagiously spread. The first one to Donna was her sister Kimberly who proclaimed, "I'm going to be an aunt!"

Right behind her was Lisa, who kept clamping her hand over her mouth, and jumping up and down. Malachi rose and strode over to the growing mass of people and extended his right hand to his son-in-law and said, "Congratulations! Now you have to take care of Donna and a little one."

Roy, not very talkative, mildly blushed. "Yes sir, I'll do my best."

Malachi then turned and looked at Kimberly. "Well, since we have had some good news, does anyone else have anything to add?"

Donna and Lisa were still rocking back and forth in a melded hug and they froze and simultaneously turned and looked at Kimberly. "Yes, is there any another news?"

Kimberly's face was overcome with shock. "About what?" But then she looked over at her guest who was now trying to fade back into the woodwork and not be noticed.

Both Donna and Lisa echoed, "Tell us more about Eric."

At that point, the look on Eric's face and his body language betrayed him showing that he wanted to be any other place than where he was right now. Kimberly walked over to him and reached out her hand to him. He wisely reciprocated her effort but did so, mostly out of fear and not knowing what he should be doing right now.

A huge smile slowly crept over Kimberly's face. "Well, if you nosy people must know, Eric and I have been dating for a while," and she paused, "well, we might be getting serious."

Malachi had since returned to his seat in the recliner but shifted his gaze rapidly toward Eric sitting to his left on the couch. "Is that true, Eric? Are you getting serious with my daughter?"

Eric found himself at a loss for words and in a mousey tone, squeaked out, "Yes, sir. I mean if that's all right sir."

Lisa moved her hand in a downward motion toward Malachi as she and Donna left their embrace and quickly mobbed Kimberly. As the trio shifted back and forth exuberantly, Malachi caught Eric's eyes and winked assuring him that he was just being teased.

Lisa stepped back from the group cuddle and caught her breath and looked over at Malachi. "Honey, we're going to be grandparents and another wedding!"

Malachi felt the same as Lisa, but he let out his expressions in a manly manner. "Yea, I guess it's good."

Both girls halted their clinch and folded their arms in protest as they yelped in stereo, "Dad!"

Lisa's eyes grew wider and she sent one of the secret wife transmissions to her husband. Malachi started laughing and stood and walked toward his daughters. "I'm just teasing you two. I am very happy for both of you." And father and daughters were gathered in a sweet bear hug.

The rest of the evening was filled with embarrassing anecdotes and stories of funny episodes that happened when the girls were growing up. Donna and Kimberly spent most of the time either rolling their eyes or trying to deny or alter the telling of the stories.

As Malachi and Lisa walked their guests out after collecting coats and jackets from their bedroom, he wrapped his arm around Lisa as they were standing on the small concrete doorstep, waving good-bye to their family. As the last car turned on the street and final waves were finished, Malachi turned to Lisa and held her close. "Thank you for being such a wonderful wife. Thank you for giving me such a beautiful family."

"And it sounds like our family is growing!"

"Yes, not only on earth but in Heaven as well."

"Honey, did you miss your dad since he wasn't at your party?"

"Yes, I did. I'm happy he's with Mom and David and our other family but I miss him."

The next couple of years just flew by. When Malachi turned sixty years old, he remembered a thought-provoking quote from one of Pastor Don's sermons, "As you get older, the days drag on but the years fly by." Malachi deeply pondered how true that statement was.

Donna and Roy's first child, Aiden, entered the world as a whirlwind and Lisa's grandmotherly energy amazed Malachi. Two years later, Kimberly and Eric stood in front of Pastor Skinner as they exchanged vows. As Malachi was walking her down the white runner stretched out on the red church carpeting, he openly wept tears of joy.

When Malachi turned sixty years old, Donna gave birth to their second child, Emily and once again, he was astounded at how Lisa pitched in and often. Both grandchildren spent much time in their house, one a toddler and the other a newborn. Lisa had stopped working and was able to be on call for her daughters, sometimes running necessary errands to the store for diapers or just to spend time with them.

The last two years of Malachi's teaching career was filled with great joy and an underlying sadness. He loved standing at the front of his classroom teaching students the military tactics of battles. He enjoyed their insight and comments as he pored over countless essays, some bringing laughter, others causing him to shake his head.

Malachi also loved the school atmosphere as after classes were over and the throngs of students disappeared, he would walk down through the silent hallways, encased with sentry-like rows of grey lockers adorned with hanging locks. Passing by the crowded cork bulletin board, Malachi quickly perused the posters of many activities and hand drawn artwork created by the students.

But the closer his retirement date was coming, the sadder he felt. Malachi knew that he wasn't as mentally sharp as he had been in his younger days and caught himself forgetting dates of historical events that he had taught many, many times before. Malachi also wondered what he was going to do with the rest of his life. Curiosity crept up through his thoughts, "What do retired people do all day?"

Instinctively, he knew that he would keep busy with his grandkids, daughters, sons-in-law, and wife but he had no idea what his new normal would look like. When Malachi retired, a celebratory party was thrown at the church and many former students stopped by the decorated fellowship hall to express their admiration and throw in some good-humored joking.

Throughout the party, Malachi caught himself glancing often at Lisa who was making sure the crystal punch bowl was filled with her special holiday recipe and issuing orders to the girls to refill the round, metal trays lined with little cut up roast beef and ham sandwiches. Malachi laughed as he saw his sons-in-law drafted into service by his wife as they lugged out overfilled black garbage bags stuffed with debris out to the blue, boxlike dumpster behind the church.

But Malachi also noticed that Lisa was not moving at her normal pace. She seemed to be slowing down a little. Now that he was sixty-five years old and she was sixty-three, they were not young at all but normally, she seemed to have much more energy. At one point, during an extended gaze, he looked over at her and it appeared that she seem weary as her face showed signs of exhaustion and her body seemed almost frail.

After they had loaded into the car after party, Malachi turned to Lisa. "Are you all right, honey?"

Normally she would respond in a chipper manner but instead replied, "I'm not sure what's going on but I just don't feel like myself lately."

"What's going on? Have you gone to your doctor?"

Lisa reached over and patted Malachi's shoulder. "I'm sure everything is fine. I'll call next week and make an appointment."

But everything was not fine.

Hospital tests were run, vials of blood taken from her body, x-rays compiled into her expanding medical file and now she and Malachi nervously sat in front of the oversized oak desk of Doctor Edgemon's office.

Doctor Edgemon had worked with the Byrges for years but as she entered the room they could tell she was bothered with the news she was about to share with them, "Malachi, Lisa, it's so good to see you two but I'm afraid I have some bad news."

Malachi deeply inhaled and Lisa sat in a still manner, almost afraid to move. Dr. Edgemon continued, "Lisa, the tests show that you have lung cancer."

Both Malachi and Lisa reached over to each other before they cognitively understood they were doing so and Lisa's spirit took on a quietness. Malachi's mind was flooded with a deluge of questions. "What does that mean? What do we have to do? Will there be treatment? Is she going to die?"

Dr. Edgemon patiently and kindly listened to all of Malachi's concerns as she looked sympathetically at Lisa. "I understand you have a lot of questions. There is some good news here. We did catch it very early so with chemotherapy and radiation treatments we believe that we can beat this."

Hope reappeared in Lisa's eyes and Malachi leaned back as Dr. Edgemon continued, "I'll be working with Dr. Strunk, an oncologist, and he'll oversee the treatments. He's a good doctor with a great deal of experience."

Malachi was trying to process everything but found the same questions racing around in his mind. "So, she's going to live, right?"

Shaking her head in affirmation, Dr. Edgemon said, "We believe so but the treatment won't be easy."

After thanking the doctor, Malachi and Lisa quietly settled into their car. Looking straight ahead, Lisa stoically stated, "Let's go to the park. You know, where you proposed."

"Absolutely."

Walking along the narrow concrete biking trail, they saw the old, beaten picnic bench Malachi proposed to Lisa so long ago. They both caught that it had suffered through the ravages of time but was still sturdy.

Lisa plopped down upon the top of the wooden table while Malachi stood before her facing her. "I guess we are like this table, hon, old, splintered but still here."

Lisa let out a brief chuckle but then immediately tears flowed from her eyes. Sobbing and shaking, she leaned into the embrace of her husband whom she loved so much. Malachi wrapped her in his arms like a fortress of safety. "You heard the doctor, we are going to beat this."

In between sobs and a torrent of tears, Lisa uttered, "I know we will. I just don't want to leave you or the kids yet."

For the longest time, Malachi swayed back and forth cradling his bride as he comforted her. As they walked back, hand in hand, toward the car, Lisa looked over at Malachi, "You were wondering what you were going to do to keep busy when you retired, well, now you know."

"I will do whatever you want me to do. I love you with all of my heart."

Those were not words of phony platitude or spoken glibly, Malachi drove Lisa to every treatment and at times, carried her into the house and gently laid her upon their bed afterwards. He cooked the meals and cleaned the house and knelt down with her on the floor beside the toilet stool when she became violently ill because of the toxic treatments.

One day as she was enduring her chemotherapy sessions, she was sitting up in bed, brushing her hair, and noticed that her once blonde hair, now graying, was coming out in clumps. Malachi was carrying a tray of chicken noodle soup in for her and he saw her staring at her plastic hairbrush in tears. Putting the tray down on the bed, he leaned over to her, "What's wrong, honey?"

Lisa tried to stop crying but couldn't. "You are doing so much for me and now, I'm losing my hair."

Malachi tenderly took the hairbrush from her hands and pretended to brush his own hair. "That's not a problem, I'll just give you some of mine."

"Honey, don't get mad at me for saying this but you don't have that much hair to give."

"You're right and if you lose all your hair, so will I."

Lisa valiantly fought through the remainder of the chemo and radiation treatments and Malachi served and ministered to her in a truly loving way. The girls pitched in and helped tremendously and their husbands joined in on the workforce and mowed the grass and took care of any household repairs that were needed.

After six long and grueling months, once again Malachi and Lisa were sitting in Dr. Edgemon's office. This time, Dr. Edgemon was smiling and said, "We believe we got it all. At this point, we can't find anymore cancer cells. Of course, we're going to see you for checkups but we believe you're going to be all right."

Both Malachi and Lisa giggled as their hands found each other and gripped themselves lovingly. Driving home later, Malachi turned to Lisa, "Let's go to the park."

"What a great idea."

Back on the familiar setting of their picnic bench, Malachi offered a prayer of thanks to the Father praising Him for the healing of his wife. Lisa, with her hands wrapped around him joined in the beautiful invocation. When they arrived home, Lisa told Malachi, "I have to tell the good news to the girls." From the living room, Malachi could hear the excitement of the girls over the phone and settled back into his recliner peacefully.

Rolling out of his bed on his sixty-sixth birthday, Malachi held his left shoulder with his right hand while making circular motions to break up the stiffness. The older Malachi was getting, the more arthritis was creeping in and there were days when Malachi's body was invaded by the nagging ache of pain.

But he was excited because he knew that he'd be able to talk to his mother. He was a little disappointed in advance because he knew this would be their last phone call but was still looking forward to it. Malachi's morning slipped by and he settled into his padded recliner awaiting the last phone call from Heaven.

At 1:17 p.m., lit up words on Malachi's phone screen flashed, "Heaven" and he didn't automatically rush to answer it because he wanted to take it all in. He just wanted to enjoy this time much like when a person has one more bite of juicy steak and they want to take their time to savor it.

Pressing the talk button, Malachi heard, "Happy Birthday to my beautiful gift from God."

"Mom, it is so good to hear from you!"

"Oh honey, I can't believe that you are sixty-six years old."

"Trust me, I can believe it. My body has more aches and pains than I have ever had before."

"Don't worry honey, there will be a day when that all is gone and your new body will be whole."

Malachi smiled and then knew that his mother would barrage him with loads of questions, which she didn't fail him. "How is Lisa? How are the girls? How are the grandkids? How was retiring? Tell me everything!"

Malachi had been prepared to provide all the information his mother was asking but he always knew that she most likely knew what he was going to say before it came from his mouth. "The girls are good. Donna now has two children and they are running around. Aiden is seven years old and asks questions all the time. Emily is five years old and will be starting kindergarten soon."

"Tell me do you have fun when they are around?"

"Oh Mom, you never would believe what those two get into. What one doesn't think of, the other one will. The other day, I caught them in the kitchen and they pushed chairs over to the counter and were getting into the sugar cannister. When I asked them what they were doing, they looked at each other and Aiden said, 'We are making cookies."

"Oh, how precious. How are the girls?"

"They're doing well. Donna and Roy just bought a house and Kimberly and Eric may be relocating because of his job but we will see."

"Oh my, that would be hard on Lisa, wouldn't it? She and the girls are close."

"Yes, it would be hard on her but it'd also be hard on me because I would miss them too."

"Yes, you would. One of the hardest things to deal with is being separated from your children. I have perfect peace and joy but there have been times when I've talked with the Father about missing you."

"What does the Father say when you talk to Him like that?"

"He reminds me how deep love reaches into our spirits and that's how much He loves us."

Malachi found himself repeating a familiar word he used when they talked about Heaven, "Wow."

"Yes, wow. So, how is Lisa?"

Malachi leaned back farther on the recliner and placed his feet on the elevated footrest. "Well, she's good now but we've had some tough times."

"What do you mean?"

"Mom, Lisa had lung cancer and had to take chemotherapy and radiation."

"I know honey. Do you remember the one night when you were so exhausted and didn't think you had the strength to keep helping her?"

Malachi wasn't trying to be funny. "Which night? I had many nights like that."

"The night you asked Donna to come over and you just got on I-69 and you drove and drove."

"I do remember that night. And it was so strange because I was frustrated and overwhelmed but after driving for a while, I felt a peace come over me."

"That's because I saw how consumed you were so I approached the Father and asked Him to send comforting angels to you."

"You did what?"

"You needed a little extra encouragement that night so a multitude of angels joined you on your drive."

"I hope they all wore seat belts."

"You have your father's humor. But I don't want you to be concerned because Lisa will never again have cancer invade her body."

Malachi bolted to a seated position. "Are you sure Mom? How do you know?"

"The Father said so and I asked His permission to share that with you."

Malachi then started to have so many images of Heaven bombard his mind. "Mom, if that's true that would make me so happy."

"Honey, it's true. If the Father says something, it is true."

"I'm sorry Mom. I wasn't questioning the Father. I still don't understand and was just trying to figure it all out."

"There you go again, trying to figure it all out."

Malachi settled back into a reclining position. "I know Mom but don't worry, I'm getting a little more introspective and accepting that I won't figure out Heaven in this lifetime."

"Honey, the Father is so incredible you'll have all eternity to figure it out."

"Mom, at times, I long to join you and Dad and David and our friends and family that are in Heaven."

"You'll be here soon enough. Enjoy those grandkids and make sure you take Tylenol when you are sore."

"Mom, the older I'm getting the more I realize how blessed I am. I guess when you're younger you are so wrapped up in what's going on that you really can't see the whole picture."

"It's true. When you are younger, life is busy. Once you get one project done, two more pop up. But as you age, you have more time to reflect."

"That's true and Mom, I've spent a lot of time reflecting."

"Yes, you have and I know you realize how blessed you are."

Malachi caught himself almost becoming weepy but stopped. "Mom, I just want you to know how thankful I am that we have been able to talk on my birthdays. Please make sure the Father knows how much I have appreciated it."

"Honey, the phone calls have made this perfect place even a little more perfect. And the Father knows how grateful you've been for the calls."

Malachi, sensing the time for the end of their conversation was drawing closer, "Mom, I hate to ask this, but will it be too much longer before I come to Heaven?"

"Now, I have told you that I can't share that with you."

Malachi, feeling like his hand was caught in the sugar jar like he caught his grandkids. "I know. I had to try."

"In the grand scheme of life, it won't be too much longer for you to be reunited with me and your father and David. But you still have plenty of time."

"Not that I'm rushing it, but I am looking forward to it."

"Honey, the next time that we talk, you'll be here in Heaven."

"I know Mom and that makes me a little sad."

"Honey, don't be sad about it but be thankful that we've been able to talk."

"You're right Mom."

Karen spoke almost in a rushed voice. "Make sure you tell Lisa and the girls and their husbands and those two sweet grand-children how much your father and I love them and don't ever forget that we are here celebrating your good times."

"And Mom when you see the hard times, the Father will show you how He'll work through them."

"You got it honey! Remember the Father loves you and your family and is working all things out for your good."

Malachi knew their last phone was ending.

"Never forget that I love you with all of my heart!"

Malachi caught himself as he leaned forward and forcefully said. "Mom, Mom. I love you too!" But he knew that the phone had gone silent.

Malachi pushed the recliner to a seated position and stood up and started pacing along the living room carpeted floor. For some reason, he felt filled with nervous energy but on the other hand, felt an overwhelming calm.

Lisa was laying down in their bedroom but heard a sound coming from the living room so she walked down their hallway and saw Malachi pacing. Peering around the corner of the wall separating the hallway from the living room, she meekly said, "Are you all right? Is it safe to come in?"

Malachi then realized what he was doing and that he had a white knuckled grip upon his phone. "Of course it's safe. I'm just a little worked up because this was the last phone call."

Lisa approached Malachi and fondly embraced him. "I know honey. Was it at least good talking to your mom one last time?"

"Yes, it was. Every phone call has been great. It's just so hard to believe it's the last one. You know she told me that the next time we talked I would be in Heaven?"

"You're not going any time soon, are you?"

"No, she told me that I have plenty of time."

"Good, because I want to spend every moment like this."

"Oh, and Mom said you would never have cancer again."

Lisa heart leapt for joy but was cautious. "I'm not doubting you honey, but did she really say that? And is she allowed to say something like that?"

"Yes, she said it and she asked the Father for permission."

"That gives me much comfort. You were so good to me through that hard time but I never want to go through that again."

Malachi echoed that sentiment. "Neither do I."

Malachi led Lisa over to their couch just adjacent to his recliner. "Honey I just want you to know that you've been the greatest wife that God has ever given anyone."

Lisa's heart was blessed. "That means so much to me. You have been the greatest husband that God could have ever given a woman."

Both Malachi and Lisa settled into one another and just enjoyed being together. So much had taken place in their lives. They stood on metaphorical mountain tops when everything just fell into place and they crawled through the darkest, lowest valleys. They shared good times and bad times. As they were entering into their last phase of life together, they wanted to appreciate their many blessings.

Malachi reached over and picked up his phone from the seat of the recliner to see his recent calls. The last one read, 'Heaven' and he fondly looked at and held it over to Lisa to see. Lisa smiled, "You really had an incredible gift from God with the phone calls."

Malachi peered at her, "You're right. I'd taken them for granted but God knew that they would eventually be greatly appreciated."

Later that night as Malachi applied toothpaste to his toothbrush, he paused and looked into the round, silver sink mirror and heard the words, "Never forget that I love you with all of my heart."

# Epilogue

T WELVE years later, Donna and Roy, their kids, Aiden and Emily, Kimberly and Eric with their only child Malachi, named after her father, and a loving wife, Lisa, were quietly huddled around Malachi's bedside. A caring hospice worker stood in the corner of their bedroom, quick to offer any assistance or help that was requested.

Malachi's breathing was labored and irregular. His family lingered with each halting breathe as Lisa tenderly caressed his hand. On the other side of the bed, Donna and Kimberly alternated holding their father's hand and when it was not their turn, wiped tears from their faces.

The frail, failing shell of Malachi's body stirred and he strained to speak one last time to his family. They had continually showered him with love expressing how much he meant to them and how thankful they were for him. Malachi's parched, tight drawn lips, struggled to open and finally, he was able to feebly utter, "Never forget that I love you all with all of my heart."

Malachi was cognizant he was dying. He felt his life force slowly leaving and was overcome with a lethargic sleepiness. He knew life was slipping from his earthly body. Then after he articulated his last words, he fell asleep.

And he went to Heaven.

When Malachi awoke, he knew he was different. He was alive. Strength and power and a force of energy coursed through him. His new imperishable, immortal body was dynamic. Gorgeous worship resounded melodically through the air as glorious sounds of praise echoed everywhere. He found himself embraced by a brighter light than he had ever seen before. The strong, eternal arms of Jesus Christ held him tighter than he had ever been held before. Security, tranquility, and love exuded from the Lamb of God and Malachi soaked it all in.

As Malachi leaned back from an embrace he would enjoy and treasure throughout all eternity, a huge smile appeared on his face as he heard these words, "There he is, my beautiful gift from God!"

www.ingramcontent.com/pod-product-compliance
Lightning Source LLC
Chambersburg PA
CBHW070815250626
47170CB00006B/2119